I FIX

By

Riano D. McFarland

7-2020
Awesome !!!

Finished Reading 8-10-20

Copyright © 2020 by Riano D. McFarland.

All rights reserved. No part of this book may be reproduced or transmitted in any form or by any means, electronic or mechanical, including photocopying, recording, or by an information storage and retrieval system, without permission in writing from the copyright owner.

This is a work of fiction. names, characters, places, and incidents either are the product of the author's imagination or are used fictitiously, and any resemblance to any actual person, living or dead, events, or locales is entirely coincidental.

Any figures depicted in stock imagery are models, and such images are being used for illustrative purposes only.

This book is dedicated to my father, Robert H. McFarland, who introduced my family to the natural wonders of Idaho while assigned to Mountain Home Air Force Base. Although it would be impossible to describe the beauty of the majestic landscapes and panoramas we explored together as a family, those images are a permanent part of my childhood memories.

The numerous hunting, fishing, and camping trips we took together were probably the reason we grew so close as a family and provided a plethora of delightful experiences that I continue to treasure even today. During the process of writing this book, I was often reminded of those magic moments in the wide-open spaces of Idaho, guided by the adventurous nature of my dad, as we tagged along behind him, attempting to follow in the footsteps of a giant.

I love you Dad!

Kim D. McFarland
5/26/2020

I FIX BROKEN THINGS

Chapter One

It was an odd name for an establishment, especially in a town like Mountain Home, Idaho. Even more unusual, was the fact that the shop seemed to have opened overnight, without so much as a single moving truck ever appearing out in front of the building. Nevertheless, promptly at 10:00 a.m. on Monday morning, the store opened, and an unusually dapper middle-aged man with a waxed mustache and tilted bowler hat, stood expectantly in the doorway, ready for business.

Unlike Boise, Idaho, Mountain Home had remained a relatively small town over the years, serving primarily as a support community for the military members and their families assigned to the Air Force Base there. While the Air Force's F-15 Eagles routinely blistered across the skies, on the ground life was much less intense, moving at a pace more attuned to the natural wonders in and around Elmore county.

Even though Mountain Home was certainly no thriving metropolis, the constant presence of US military cutting edge weapons systems and technology along with the personnel required to keep it in a constant state of readiness, made the otherwise small northwestern city, far from an isolated backwater Cowtown.

While it's logical you'd find people in any sized city who'd eventually need repair services of some kind or another, it would certainly seem difficult to base an entire business model on such a rapidly diminishing market niche. With superstores and mega-market centers slinging products out the door at ridiculously low prices, it was becoming more and more convenient to completely replace broken or damaged products, than it was to actually have them repaired.

Despite the market realities to be considered, there it was... right at the intersection of North Main and East Jackson streets across from Railroad Park. Added to its list of other oddities, there didn't seem to be any particular category of "broken" things which their expertise specifically addressed. Unlike wristwatch or electronics repair shops, the establishment's name was curiously vague.

Perhaps it was the non-specific nature of the shop which piqued Amanda's curiosity. Even though she couldn't think of anything, off hand, she needed serviced, that didn't stop her from wanting to take a look inside. Actually, it didn't take much to draw Amanda's attention towards anything. For some people, she might even be considered nosey, but sometimes things required closer scrutiny, and for such occasions, Amanda was more than willing to serve as the community's non-elected public investigator. After all, who's to say when something ordinary could turn out to be dangerous?

As she briskly walked toward the shop, she was somewhat taken aback when the door opened while she was extending her hand to grasp the doorknob. Just inside the doorway, she was greeted by a smiling gentleman who seemed more suited to an era gone by; however, his smile was genuine as was the immediate sense of comfort she felt upon stepping across the threshold and into the surprisingly large but cluttered shop.

"Mrs. Witherspoon!" said the shopkeeper in a voice filled with confidence and enthusiasm. "How nice of you to stop by this morning!"

Squinting suspiciously, she said, "I'm sorry Sir, but have we met? I don't recall having made your acquaintance."

Without even acknowledging the question revealing her obvious paranoia, the shopkeeper asked, "What might I fix for you today?"

Unprepared for his innocuous yet direct question, she was a bit taken aback, stammering "Well, I... uh... actually, I..."

"Oh, I quite understand." interjected the shopkeeper. "It's often difficult to express oneself concerning such 'intimate' matters."

The way he'd leaned in before nearly whispering the words 'intimate matters' left Amanda a bit confused. There was obviously no one other than the two of them inside the shop, so his unnecessary insinuation of the need for secrecy seemed unwarranted.

9

"What do you mean?" she stammered indignantly. "I have nothing of the sort requiring your services."

"Oh, Mrs. Witherspoon, It's alright. All repairs are handled with the utmost discretion," replied the curious gentleman. "But please... take your time to think it over, and when you're ready, simply come back with what's broken, and I'll fix it for you," he added with a smile, as he ushered her back towards the exit.

"How do you know my name?" asked Amanda, obviously irritated. "We've never met."

"Of course, we have, Mrs. Witherspoon," answered the gentleman with such a curiously disarming smile. "Your signature is on my business license right next to the front door."

Now, more perplexed than ever, she peered over her horn-rimmed glasses squinting as she scrutinized the framed document hanging on the wall next to the door. Sure enough, her unmistakable signature adorned the lower right-hand corner of the license. The document was dated only three days earlier on the Friday preceding the weekend which had just wrapped up.

"I... don't recall..." she stammered.

"It's quite alright, Mrs. Witherspoon. Someone with your busy schedule couldn't possibly remember everyone who appears at your service window in City Hall," said the smiling gentleman, gesturing as if to dismiss the entire matter.

As he opened the door for her, she turned to him, asking "What did you say your name was again, Mr...?"

"Abernathy. Malcolm Abernathy," stated the man with a smile, before adding "Please come again whenever you're ready."

Before she could even respond, he closed the door behind her. Turning back to look into the shop window, he was nowhere to be seen.

As she got into her car, she couldn't help but feel he'd nearly kicked her out, in possibly the most courteous manner she'd ever experienced. During the short drive home, and for the remainder of the evening, she couldn't seem to get the strange visit out of her mind. Even as she lay in bed trying to sleep that night, her mind was racing, attempting to identify something she could take to the store for repair.

Hours later, while rummaging through the attic, of all places, she came across an old wooden chest. While she recognized it immediately, she hadn't opened it in nearly fifty years. The chest had been at the foot of the double bed shared by Amanda and her little sister, Kaitlyn.

Before she even opened it, she knew what she would find inside. After pausing for a moment, she flipped up the dusty brass latches and opened the chest. As expected, the tin red, yellow, and blue toy spinning top was the first thing that caught her eye.

Carefully removing it from the chest, she placed it on the floor beside her. Pulling up the spiral stemmed pump at the top of the toy, she pushed it down to the crackling sound of what seemed to be misaligned gears which couldn't connect to something inside the sealed tin exterior anymore. As a result, the toy, while in pristine condition on the outside, simply did not work anymore.

As children, Amanda and Kaitlyn had a two-year age gap, and personalities which were as different as day and night. Amanda was certainly the more daring and adventurous of the two, always looking for some new adrenalin rush, while Kaitlyn could spend hours happily engrossed in her coloring books.

Kaitlyn had received the spinning top as a gift on her sixth birthday and immediately fallen in love with it. She literally spent hours every single day lying on the floor next to it watching it spin, claiming it was her spaceship, and that eventually, she was going to get a real one and fly away inside it.

Amanda thought the idea was ridiculous, calling Kaitlyn stupid for even thinking such a thing. Of course, Kaitlyn couldn't have cared less, as she watched her top spinning nearly as fast as her imagination.

Of all the things Amanda found irritating, being ignored by her younger sister was at the top of the list. Purely out of spite, she forcefully kicked Kaitlyn's favorite toy, sending it sailing into the wall. Kaitlyn scampered across the floor and picked it up. Shaking it, she could hear something rattling around inside, and when she attempted to use the pump and set it in motion again, the crunching sound coming from inside it was as telling as the tears streaking down her little face.

"You broke it!" cried Kaitlyn "Now I'll never be able to fly!"

Amanda immediately realized she'd gone too far, and that their mom was going to launch into another of her infamous tirades if she found out what happened. Attempting to calm Kaitlyn, she said, "I didn't mean to. It was an accident!"

"You did it on purpose!" said Kaitlyn. "It was my favorite thing in the whole world, and you broke it..."

As Kaitlyn's words trailed off into tearful sobs, she curled herself around the broken toy, there on the floor.

Finally comprehending the damage, she had done, she walked over to her little sister and sat down on the floor beside her. Despite Kaitlyn's protest, she lifted her sisters head onto her lap, caressing her hair and wiping the tears from her eyes. "I'm sorry Kaitlyn. I was only jealous because I thought you loved your top more than you love me."

"I love you more than anything Mandy," said Kaitlyn softly. "I just wanted to fly so much!" she added, breaking into tears all over again.

"You can't really fly with a spinning top, Kaitlyn," said Amanda.

"I know that," said Kaitlyn, "but, if I laid down on the floor next to it while it was spinning, I could close my eyes and really imagine that I was flying."

Suddenly, Amanda had an idea. "I can show you how it feels to really fly, if you want me to!" she said.

"Really?" asked her little sister. "How?"

Taking the broken top and placing it inside the toy chest, she closed the lid before taking Kaitlyn's hand. "Come on!" said Amanda. "I'll show you!"

Together, they rushed down the stairs and out the back door. Across from the field behind their house was a small park with a seesaw, a merry-go-round, some monkey bars, and a swing-set. Giggling loudly, they both sprinted through the tall grass and over to the park, hand-in-hand.

They stopped in front of the swing-set, where Amanda said "Get on Kaitlyn. I'll push you!"

"How do I do it?" asked Kaitlyn.

"Just sit on the seat and hold onto the chains with both hands. When I push forward, you lean back and kick your feet forward. On the way back, you tuck your feet underneath and lean forward," explained Amanda. "The harder you kick, the higher you can fly!"

"Really!?" said Kaitlyn, excitedly. "Show me!"

Amanda helped her climb into the seat, saying "Now, hold on tight when I push, okay?"

"Okay!" said Kaitlyn excitedly.

It took a little while for Kaitlyn to get the hang of it as Amanda began pushing the swing, but pretty soon, she was able to coordinate her leg positions with the swing's motion, and before long, both girls were laughing loudly, as Kaitlyn swung higher and higher.

"Push harder, Mandy! I'm really flying!" said the little girl, kicking her feet forward harder and harder with each subsequent swing. For Kaitlyn, it was the most amazing sensation she'd ever known.

"That's high enough, Kaitlyn," said Amanda. "I don't want you to fall off," she added with a smile.

"Higher Mandy! Just a little bit higher!" said the excited little girl seconds before the loop holding the chain at the top of the swing snapped.

At 10:00 a.m. sharp, Amanda Witherspoon was standing at the door of Mr. Abernathy's shop. Her eyes were hidden behind dark sunglasses, and in her hands, she held the broken top close to her chest.

"Ah, Mrs. Witherspoon," he said, smiling compassionately as he opened the door to welcome her inside. "I see you've found it after all."

Without a word, he took the broken toy from her and invited her to have a seat across from him at the ancient looking, heavy wooden workbench. As he retrieved a small tool kit from the shelf behind him, Amanda looked around the shop, drinking in the assortment of oddities populating the shelves of the somewhat mysterious locale.

Sitting down across from her at the sturdy workbench, he said "This is one of the rarer versions of this toy. An amazing piece actually. They've been built in exactly the same way for a couple of centuries now," he explained.

"The top works by turning reciprocal motion into rotational motion around the toy's natural axis," he said. "The only really vulnerable part is the fitted washer around the spiral plunger. Once they started using plastic instead of steel, it didn't take much to damage them. In fact, they would wear out after a while, simply from being used as they were intended to be."

Opening the top, he removed the plastic washer and held it up to the light over his workbench. "This one looks like it was used very often," he said. "You see... here around the plunger stem, the plastic washer was completely worn out. It simply couldn't grip the stem anymore."

"Yes," said Amanda. "Kaitlyn used to play with it for hours and hours each and every day," said Amanda with a nostalgic smile. "It was her favorite toy in the whole world."

"Well, it was only a matter of time before it stopped working after that kind of use," said Mr. Abernathy.

"I broke it by accident," said Amanda. "It was my fault. I kicked it into a wall and broke it."

"No, Mrs. Witherspoon... You didn't," said Mr. Abernathy. "The plastic fitting which grips the spiral plunger was completely worn out. If things rub against each other long enough, they will eventually wear through one another. Your sister must have really loved this toy, because the opening inside this plastic washer is oval shaped when it should actually be square. There's no way kicking it could have caused this. No way at all," he said. Looking up at her, he added "It wasn't your fault."

"But it was!" sobbed Amanda. "It had to have been, because had I not kicked it, we wouldn't have ever gone to that park, and Kaitlyn wouldn't have fallen off of the swing!" she said as the floodgates, welded shut for so long, finally opened to release the emotions which had been trapped inside her for nearly half a century.

Placing his hand on Amanda's shoulder, he said "Mrs. Witherspoon, this toy was worn out because Kaitlyn loved it so much; not because you kicked it."

When she looked up at him, Mr. Abernathy was holding the top. Placing it on the table between them, he pumped the stem, sending it into the rotation she so clearly remembered from her childhood.

Suddenly, she remembered the anguish she felt as her little sister's body had lain there in the grass, motionless. The chain had broken at the apex of her flight, propelling her out and away from the swing where she landed at an awkward angle, instantly snapping her neck.

Her parents, the paramedics, the police, and numerous psychiatrists tried for years to ease her feelings of guilt, explaining how the hooks and chains on the swing set had simply worn through one another, and that it was in no way her fault.

Still, Amanda had carried the burden of that broken tin top through her entire life, and into the front door of Mr. Abernathy's shop. As he escorted her to the door, she stopped and turned to face him, asking "By the way, how much do I owe you?"

"For five minutes of work, and a ten-cent metal washer... I couldn't possibly charge you anything," he said with a smile.

As he walked her out to her car, an F-15 fighter aircraft streaked loudly across the clear blue-sky drawing both of their gazes skyward.

Shaking her head, Amanda said "I don't understand how those fighter pilots do it. They could crash or be shot down every time they get into the cockpit."

"Yes," said Mr. Abernathy, handing the toy spinning top back to her. "But before they crash... they get to fly."

With that, Mr. Abernathy said "Good day, Mrs. Witherspoon," before turning and disappearing back inside his peculiar little shop.

On her way home, Amanda Witherspoon stopped by the post office where she mailed a check made out to, *I FIX BROKEN THINGS*. In the memo, she'd written "My Soul".

It was for one-thousand dollars.

Chapter Two

Mr. Abernathy's shop reminded Peter of a traveling salesman's wagon from the mid-1800s. He actually expected to walk into a shop filled with bottles of undefined elixirs which claimed to cure every ailment from cold sores to cancer. Upon meeting the proprietor in person, this preconception was further cemented into place, whether justly or unjustly.

"Good afternoon, Sir," came the enthusiastic greeting from Mr. Abernathy. "What can I fix for you today?"

Looking around, mostly out of curiosity, Peter replied "To be honest with you, I just wanted to check out the place. It reminds me of something from the cowboy days."

"Hmmm..." replied Mr. Abernathy. "I didn't realize cowboys were an extinct species," he said with a smile.

"Oh, you know what I mean," said Peter. "It's like a throwback to a simpler time, when every town had a blacksmith, a cobbler, a tailor, or a gunsmith who fixed things and kept them going for generations instead of only until the batteries died in them."

"Yes, I do understand how someone could get that impression," said Mr. Abernathy. "Although, to be accurate, it wasn't necessarily a simpler time. In fact, it was a much more complicated era, requiring everyone inside a community to interact for the sake of keeping things in balance. If there was a fire, everyone grabbed a bucket. If a barn was raised, everyone tugged a rope."

"True," said Peter as he continued on his browsing tour. "I never really thought about it from that point of view."

"Well, let me know if you think of anything, I can fix for you," replied Mr. Abernathy before disappearing into an office off to the side of the shop.

Peter found it odd, that there were so many items on the shelves of a shop who's stated purpose was to fix broken things, not to sell them. However, as he continued perusing the oddities on the shelves, he realized there were no price tags on anything, begging the question, why were there so many items on the shelves inside a store that didn't actually sell anything?

"Sometimes the question is the answer," came the shopkeeper's voice from directly behind him.

"What?" asked Peter, slightly confused by the audible answer to his unspoken question.

"I could tell by the way you were looking around, that you were wondering why I have so many items on the shelves in a store that doesn't really seem to sell anything," explained Mr. Abernathy. "I get that a lot," he added with a smile.

"It is a curious observation," said Peter.

"Sometimes, people don't remember they have things in need of repair until they see the same or similar items on the shelves here," explained Mr. Abernathy. "They simply push things further and further back into their own shelves, planning on eventually getting around to fixing them, but soon get distracted and never come back to them."

"So, you just collect this stuff without even knowing if you'll ever have a use for it?" asked Peter.

"For every forgotten thing pushed to the back of a shelf, there's someone out there willing to put in the work needed to fix it. Sooner or later, those things will wind up here and I'll put them back together, even if I don't plan on using them myself," said the peculiar shopkeeper.

Peter smiled inwardly, thinking how absurd it was for such a person to call themselves anything but a hoarder. Most everything he noticed in the shop was old, outdated, obsolete, or useless and he couldn't imagine why anyone would even want to collect such odds and ends. As he turned to walk back towards the front door, something caught and held his gaze.

Peter had been an engineer for years, designing complex equipment for the aeronautics and automobile industries. After designing an ejection survival pod for naval fighter aircraft, he started his own engineering and design firm, attracting clients from all over the world who incorporated his design into their next generation fighter jets.

Even though he didn't really need the money anymore, he would still spend hours working, in search of the next big thing despite already owning the patents on a system which would undoubtedly be a substantial source of income for the next century. In the meantime, his wife and kids were constantly badgering him about finding time to slow down, relax, and enjoy the fruits of his success.

One evening, during an argument with his wife Anna, over quality time, he carelessly knocked an antique music box from the dresser onto the hardwood floor in the bedroom. While there was only minimal damage to the box itself, it couldn't play music anymore.

It was the first gift he'd ever given his wife, and while he didn't assign much significance to it, Anna was heartbroken. Attempting to calm her, he apologized profusely and promised to fix it for her the next day. That day came and went four years earlier, and he'd completely forgotten the music box downstairs in his workshop collecting dust.

Peter did an astonished double-take when he saw a what appeared to be an identical music box on the shelf to his left. "Where did you get this?" he asked, attempting to estimate the odds of randomly finding such an item in a store which had only opened a couple of weeks ago.

Smiling, Mr. Abernathy said, "A young woman brought it in a week or so ago. I fixed it while she waited, and when it was done, she paid for the repair, but decided not to take it with her. She told me that perhaps it would be better if she just forgot about it and moved on."

Peter lifted the box from the shelf to look it over. On the bottom, there was a handwritten sticker bearing the name Anna. Turning to the shopkeeper, he asked "What was wrong with it?"

"Oh, nothing that anyone with an X-Acto knife, a drop of wood glue, and ten minutes of extra time, couldn't have fixed," answered Mr. Abernathy. "One of the cogs connecting the metal spring to the music mechanism popped off. Once I'd cut along the bottom seam and moved the felt lining aside, I saw the problem right away. I used the same knife to put the gear back in place and sealed it up with a dab of Elmer's. Now, it's good as new."

"How much are you asking for it?" asked Peter.

"Oh, I couldn't sell that," said Mr. Abernathy. "Since she's already paid for it, the client still owns it... even though it's still here in my store. I'll hold it for another forty-five days, and if she doesn't pick it up, I'll consider it abandoned and then I'd be happy to sell it to you."

Noticing the concerned look in the young man's eyes, Mr. Abernathy said "People assign significance to the strangest things, while a beautiful piece like that gets neglected and abandoned. When you stop appreciating something beautiful, you simply leave the door open for someone else, who will see the beauty you no longer notice. After that, it's only a matter of time before it winds up in someone else's hands."

Suddenly, Peter was in a hurry to leave. He left the shop without another word, jumped straight into his truck, and sped off down the street. Fifteen minutes later, he was pulling into the driveway of his lavish ranch-style home. At the house, there was a late model pickup truck parked under the trees near the gate which led to the back yard, out of view from the main road.

Quietly opening the front door, he entered the foyer without making a sound, silently making his way down the hallway towards the kitchen. There were two glasses containing melting ice on the countertop, both with condensation rings formed around the base. Draped across the back of one of the barstools near the patio door, was a man's shirt.

Peter was blind with jealous rage, as he left the kitchen and crept down the hallway to the study, where he removed a handgun from the bottom drawer of his desk. With the gun in his hand, he solemnly walked toward the master bedroom at the opposite end of the house. He slowed as he approached, noticing the door was slightly ajar.

The sense of dread he felt in the pit of his stomach was nearly overwhelming as he slowly pushed the door open and peered inside. In the corner of the bedroom, his wife was sitting in the armchair near the window where she would often enjoy the view of the horse stables off in the distance. There was an open book on the blanket across her lap and she was napping peacefully.

As if sensing his presence, she slowly opened her eyes and smiled, saying "Hi Honey. I wasn't expecting you to be home so soon today."

As her vision slowly cleared, she noticed the pistol in her husband's hand and asked, "What's going on Sweetheart? Why do you have the gun in your hand?" Suddenly, her eyes widened, and she sprang to her feet, asking "Are the kids alright!?"

Peter's blank stare evaporated as if he were emerging from a thick fog. Upon seeing her asleep in the chair, he'd forgotten all about the gun in his hand and the imaginary affair he was expecting to stumble into.

Suddenly, she was right in front of him, asking "Honey, is everything alright?!" clearly worried about their children.

"No. Yes... yes," he stammered. "The kids are fine," he added, placing the gun on top of the chest of drawers and wrapping his arms around his wife, who's whole body was trembling as he held her.

From down the hallway, they heard a voice calling out, "Mrs. Williams, I'm finished with the pool. I'll leave through the back gate and see you again next Thursday."

"That's fine," said Anna, adding "The money is in the envelope beneath the magnet on the refrigerator."

"Thank you, Ma'am," said the man from down the hallway before sliding the patio door closed behind him. A few seconds later, his truck rumbled to life and could be heard heading down the lane to the front gate of the property and turning onto the highway.

Walking hand-in-hand, the two of them made their way into the kitchen, taking a seat at the counter. The shirt which had been across the back of the barstool was gone, and one of the two glasses had been rinsed out and was drying in the dishrack near the sink.

Looking at Anna, Peter said "You know... I've been thinking. You and the kids are right. We should take a few days to get away from here. Maybe load up the camper and surprise the kids with a trip up to Lake Brownlee for the weekend."

"That would be wonderful Peter; but, what about the contracts you're working on for the British Navy? Are you sure you can just get away right now? I know how hard you work for me and the kids, and I don't want to take you away from something that important."

Looking at Anna, Peter said "Actually, this is something that's long overdue. I've been pushing and pushing and had almost forgotten the reason I've worked so hard. It was so that I *could* have time to spend with my family before we're too old, or too sick to enjoy it anymore."

"Then, yes!" said Anna, excitedly. "Let's do it, and we won't say anything to the kids until tomorrow morning when I'd normally wake them for school."

"That's an excellent idea!" exclaimed Peter. "I'll prepare everything tonight after they're in bed, and we'll set out first thing in the morning."

Looking into his eyes, Anna said "I love you Sweetheart. Thank you for taking some time to spend alone with us. It's something I think we're all in need of."

Nodding, Peter kissed her and smiled just before he heard the school bus stopping out at the end of the lane to drop off Amy and Aaron.

Later that evening, after the kids were in bed and fast asleep, Peter went into the basement downstairs to fuel up the lanterns and grab some fishing gear for their early-morning trip to Lake Brownlee. As he was about to turn off the light over his workbench, he noticed the music box on the shelf, right behind his mp3-player. Directly beside it was an X-Acto knife and a small bottle of wood glue.

    Chuckling to himself, he sat down at the bench with the music box in front of him. Using the knife, he carefully separated the felt lining from the bottom of the music box and pulled it aside, immediately spotting the dislocated cog. With the same knife, he placed it back onto the spindle and popped it firmly into place. Afterwards, he put a drop of glue on his fingertip and spread it evenly along the edge of the felt liner and held it in place against the side of the music box for a few seconds, letting it dry.

    Winding the spring with the key on the back of the box, he placed in on the bench and opened the top, filling the room with music which had been absent for far too long. When he closed the lid and picked up the box, he turned to find Anna there smiling at him.

    "I thought you'd forgotten about that thing," said Anna.

    "Honestly," said Peter "I had. I'd gotten so accustomed to fixing big things, that I forgot it was the little things that
used to make us smile the most."

    Handing it back to her, he said "Here you go, and it only took four years and ten minutes to fix." Smiling, he added "Maybe it wasn't the box that needed fixing after all."

    As they walked down the hallway to the master bedroom, Anna asked "Hey, have you seen that new shop across the street from Railroad Park? It looks kind of neat in an odd sort of way. We should stop in and take a look sometime."

"You know," said Peter. "Earlier today, I was thinking the exact same thing..."

Chapter Three

Malcolm Abernathy had always been a tinkerer, interested in how things worked from the inside out. Even as a young man, he'd drag things back to his parents' yard where he'd disassemble them and analyze the way the internal components fit and worked together. By the time he was twenty years old, there weren't many things he hadn't either repaired, or scavenged parts from, to use in repairing something completely different.

It wasn't only about making money for him. He'd decided long ago that he would most likely never be a wealthy man. What he found most appealing was the mindset of the people who attached meaning to objects, and how the well-being of those soulless things could influence the demeanor of the living, breathing human beings who owned them.

Some people felt that if they could restore an object to the state it was in at a particular high point in their lives, then they could somehow rediscover and reclaim the happiness associated with that object. In repairing people's "things" he could often gain insight into their individual mindsets, revealing their true character, and even... their darkest secrets.

Marcus Hamilton was the youngest of three siblings, having been born nearly ten years after his sister, who was the middle child. Throughout his childhood, he felt awkward due to the age gap;

primarily because his brother and sister treated him more like a nephew than a younger sibling and would exclude him from nearly all of their extracurricular activities. As a result, he'd spent lots of time with his father while his brother and sister were out carousing with their peers.

Marcus's dad was a very smart, hard-working man who sought to instill his work ethic into all of his children. Because Marcus was so much younger, he was able to take advantage of the additional time his father had after his retirement from the fire department. While at times, Marcus was assumed to be a grandchild rather than a son, that never really mattered to him.

Unlike his brother and sister, he could build a campfire without matches or a lighter. He could tie the mooring hitch knots for his dad at the dock and knew the difference between the starboard and port sides of the boat. Above all, Marcus listened and attempted to absorb everything. His dad was a virtual cornucopia of knowledge and knew so much about so many things, he could communicate with anyone about anything, anywhere at any time and never be at a loss for the appropriate words to define the situation. Furthermore, he was always impeccably dressed, rarely if ever being seen in public without his trademark vest. You could always see the gold chain dangling from the watch inside the right pocket and connected to the third button from the bottom of his vest.

Marcus had always been fascinated by the watch. To him, it appeared to be an almost mythical object, which gave his dad the power to be anywhere at least five minutes early. He'd check it several times a day, and you would never see him leave the house without it. When others would chuckle at the fact he hadn't ever upgraded to a wristwatch, he'd politely counter by saying "We'll see how many wristwatches you go through before this pocket watch quits."

Invariably, he was always correct and even if it took a decade, eventually those touted wristwatches proved no match for the Rolex® he'd received at his retirement ceremony. Long after his brother joined the Air Force, sporting a different watch every time he visited to go hunting and fishing with them while on leave, his dad's watch remained a constant companion and a testimony to the art of fine craftsmanship.

It was a very cold October morning when Marcus and his father left the house to go deer hunting. He'd just turned twelve a month earlier, so this would be the first time Marcus could legally hunt with his dad, and he'd tossed and turned in bed all night from the anticipation.

His mom awoke early to prepare a hearty breakfast for her two "men", and stood on the porch afterwards, waving to them as they drove off together in their old pickup. The entire time, Marcus's dad coached him, explaining how deer *hunting* was actually more like deer *waiting* because it was best to find a spot where the deer would most likely come to you.

Deer are very alert and skittish animals with keen senses of hearing and smell. At the first sign of danger, even a large six-point buck could quickly disappear into a tangle of woods and escape before a hunter could even get the crosshairs on him. Smart hunters would always look for an elevated vantage point overlooking high traffic areas frequented by big game.

After finding a secluded spot for Marcus, his father would walk up the trail a bit further, telling him "This way, we'll see them coming through, no matter which direction they approach from."

In order to avoid mistaking one another for game, which could result in a tragic hunting accident, both Marcus and his father carried police whistles. Once a shot was taken at a deer, whether it connected or not, the hunt was essentially over for the day, because the rest of the game would scatter and avoid the entire area until the coast seemed clear again. Therefore, in order to avoid being mistaken for a fleeing deer, before walking towards one another each hunter would signal their approach using the police whistle. It was a simple but effective means of eliminating accidents.

Barely fifteen minutes after taking up his position, he heard a shot ring out from over the rise where his father had burrowed in. Five seconds later, another shot rang out and then another. Listening closely, Marcus realized the sound of the gunshot wasn't that of a 30.06 rifle. It was the distinct sound of his dad's sidearm; a Colt 1911 45ACP Government Model he carried with him nearly as frequently as the pocket watch in his vest.

Tossing aside the camouflaged poncho wrapped around him, he began moving in the direction of the gunfire. Blowing fiercely into the police whistle, he was flat out running when he crested the ridge. Fifty yards down the slope in front of him, he saw the dying grizzly gasping loudly as the life drained from his punctured lungs. Sticking out from beneath the dying bear, were the legs of his father!

Throwing caution to the wind, Marcus raced down the slope to where the deathmatch had been waged, unsure of whether or not there had even been a victor. As he drew closer, he noticed his dad's legs moving as he tried to free himself from beneath the dying behemoth which had collapsed on top of him.

Standing beside them, Marcus tried to pull the bear's body off of his father. Failing at that, he sat on the ground with his back against a tree and used his legs to push against the massive animal. Finally, the combined efforts of Marcus and his dad were enough to lift the bear allowing his father to squeeze out from underneath it.

The damage resulting from the clash of these two titans had obviously been equally meted out, with neither of them escaping the horrific melee unscathed. Using his hunting knife, he cut the poncho into strips and made tourniquets for his father's left arm and leg; both of which were literally hanging by their tendons. He'd also been mauled, with deep claw marks across his back, chest, and abdomen.

Marcus covered the wounds with bandages cut from the camouflaged blanket his father had used to keep warm while dug into his perch. Finally, he folded the remainder of the blanket together, rolling his father briefly onto his side and placing it beneath the bandaged wounds on his back. In order to keep pressure on both wounds simultaneously, he lifted a large flat stone and placed it on top of the bandage covering his father's chest wound. In order to make sure there was enough pressure to slow the bleeding, he placed additional stones on top of the flat one to increase the weight as much as he dared, to avoid further injuring his dad.

Once he'd tended to his father's wounds, he reloaded the blood covered handgun with a magazine from the gun belt. There were three nine-round magazines, so Marcus would be able to send out three unmistakable messages to someone, hopefully close enough to hear them, and smart enough to know what they meant.

Pointing the massive handgun at a large tree a few feet away, he fired three shots quickly, followed by three shots slowly, and finally three shots quickly again. After reloading, he continued the same pattern of shots into the tree two additional times before the handgun ammunition was exhausted.

He still had ammunition for both his and his father's rifles, which he would use should they be confronted by another animal seeking to harm them. Taking one of the rounds, he pried the bullet out of the brass casing and poured the gunpowder inside it onto another flat rock lying on the ground a few feet away from his father. Covering the gunpowder with dry leaves and small twigs, he combed the ground until he found some dry chert stones he then used as flint to ignite a fire. Within minutes the fire was both warming the area around his dad and sending greyish-white smoke into and above the tree canopy overhead.

As luck would have it, a game warden had been patrolling the area, checking permits and deer tags as hunting season commenced. He was the first to hear the SOS trumpeted into the forest by twenty-seven rounds fired from that Colt 1911. After calling for backup, he immediately began moving in the direction of the gunfire and before long, he could smell the smoke coming from Marcus's campfire.

When the game warden appeared atop the rise above Marcus's location, he was totally unprepared for the horrific sight that greeted him. The body of the dead grizzly, the severely mauled man with tourniquets applied and stones stacked on top of his chest, and a twelve-year-old boy covered in the blood of both, standing there keeping watch over his father.

Within an hour of the attack, Marcus was with his father in the back of an ambulance on the way to the emergency room. Upon arrival, Marcus was treated for shock while a surgical team operated on his father. Half an hour later, his mother and sister arrived bewildered after receiving a call from the emergency room triage attendant.

The game warden greeted them in the ER waiting room and explained what had apparently happened in the woods earlier that morning. The paramedics who responded to the call were amazed at the quality of first aid Marcus had administered, stating that even trained emergency medical technicians could not have improved upon the care he'd provided. Furthermore, how a severely mauled man and a young teenage boy had managed to move a grizzly weighing nearly eight-hundred pounds was simply beyond all explanation.

Although Marcus's dad did eventually make it home, the injuries he suffered were ultimately too much for him to recover from. He died at home surrounded by his loved ones barely a month after being released from the hospital, but not before he could tell Marcus how proud he was of him and give him the Rolex® pocket watch he'd cherished and carried with him for so many years.

During his battle with the grizzly the crystal face of the watch had cracked, and the bezel had come loose, but for Marcus it was the most beautiful thing he could ever have received from the father he'd so deeply loved and admired. Even broken and stained with bear's blood, it was priceless to him.

It had been nearly twenty years since his father had passed on, but the lessons he taught Marcus during the time they'd spent together were enduring. While his siblings apparently had no interest in building a future for themselves and their families, Marcus was diligent and dedicated.

Only five years after losing his father, his mother fell ill and simply lacked the will to go on anymore. The doctors called it dementia, but Marcus knew she'd died of a broken heart.

Within days, both his brother and sister were at each other's throats, fighting over an inheritance neither of them could responsibly manage. Since Marcus was still a minor, his brother and sister were given shared powers of attorney over their parents' estate, and by Marcus's eighteenth birthday, every bit of it had been squandered away.

Marcus, on the other hand, remained dedicated to the pursuit of knowledge, even though he had to work two jobs in order to put himself through college at Idaho State University. After earning his Bachelor of Science in Earth and Environmental Systems, he went to work for the Forestry Service. Even though he realized it was unlikely he'd ever be a millionaire in such a career field, it was what he really loved, and he approached it with a passion he hoped would have made his father proud.

Although Marcus was the youngest of the three siblings, he was the one who's phone rang at 2:00 a.m. when his brother or sister needed another loan, or someone to post bail for their public drunkenness and intoxicated driving offenses. He tried hard to keep them above water, while slowly drowning himself in debt. Eventually, they cut ties with *him* when he had to start denying their requests.

After the bank issued a foreclosure notice on his severely over-leveraged home, he was in the attic going through his belongings trying to decide what to load into the moving truck he'd rented. While he hated having to place his personal belongings in a storage unit, he was out of options and needed time to figure out what to do next.

Suddenly, there it was. The pocket watch, he'd always drawn strength from, remembering the tenacity of his dad, even in the most austere of times. For years, it had been his sincere intention to have it repaired and restored to its original glory. He kept it in a lockbox with his passport, educational documents, and insurance certificates, considering it more important than any of the other items inside it.

On a whim, he removed the watch from the lockbox and carried it downstairs to the garage where he got into his banged up, clunker of a car and drove over to the repair shop that had recently opened up downtown on North Main. When he pulled into the parking lot, he was unsure whether or not they would even be able to fix something like an old pocket watch.

Mr. Abernathy was there to open the door for him as he approached, offering his enthusiastic salutation, saying "Welcome, kind sir. What can I fix for you today?"

"I don't know," replied Marcus. "I'm not even sure it *can* be fixed," he added, extending the pocket watch to the oddly cheerful gentleman wearing a vest reminiscent of his father's.

"Well, come in... come in!" said Mr. Abernathy. "Let's have a look-see."

Offering Marcus, a seat at the prehistoric looking workbench in the center of the store, he disappeared between the shelves near the back of the shop, returning with a box of precision watchmaker's tools.

After placing the toolbox on the table, he picked up the watch, eying it through the huge magnifying glass mounted to the table.

"This is a rare piece of exquisite craftsmanship," stated Mr. Abernathy. "I have only seen one other pocket watch in my entire life which even comes close, when compared to this one!" he added, excitedly. "Where on Earth did you find it?"

"My father gave it to me shortly before he died," answered Marcus. "Growing up, I can't remember ever seeing him without it."

"I can only imagine," said Mr. Abernathy. "This is a Rattrapante. It is one of the rarest pocket watches ever manufactured by Rolex®."

"Really?" said Marcus. "When you say rare... how rare do you mean?" he queried.

"There were only eight of them *ever* made; possibly nine, and only five of those were ever offered for sale to the general public," replied Mr. Abernathy.

"Can you restore it for me?" asked Marcus.

"I can replace the cracked lens while you wait, but there seems to be something preventing the case back from fully closing. Let's take a look and see what's going on inside there."

Carefully removing the back from the watch case, Mr. Abernathy's eyes nearly popped out of their sockets and his jaw went completely slack. Using a pair of precision surgical tweezers, he removed the object which had prevented the case from sealing properly. It was a penny.

Not quite believing his eyes, Mr. Abernathy held the penny beneath the magnifying glass, carefully scrutinizing it from every possible angle on both sides, while apparently holding his breath. When he exhaled, he said "This is a 1943-D Lincoln penny!"

The perplexed look on Marcus's face made it obvious to Mr. Abernathy, that he may as well have been speaking Latin. Carefully laying the penny back inside the watch cover, he dashed into his office, returning with a book depicting rare coins minted in the United States.

Donning white cotton gloves before touching the coin, Malcolm picked it up and placed it on the page next to the penny depicted inside the book, saying "You see, Sir. This is your penny.".

"Yes, it's definitely the same as the one shown here, but what does that mean?" asked Marcus.

Raising a single finger, he silenced Marcus. Before saying anything, he quickly replaced the cracked watch crystal and reattached the back, which now closed and sealed quite easily. Then, he cleaned and buffed the exterior, revealing the watches original luster before placing it inside a lined, padded box and sliding it across the table to Marcus.

Next, Mr. Abernathy stood up and reached inside the cabinet behind him, producing two glasses and a bottle of cognac. After pouring two fingers worth into each glass, he slid one of *them* across the table over to Marcus as well.

"Sir, which would you like to hear first; the amazing news or the fantastic news?" asked Mr. Abernathy.

"Let's start with the amazing news," said Marcus, trembling with anticipation.

"As I mentioned earlier, the watch your father gave you, is one of only eight ever manufactured. The amazing news is that it is one of the three which were never offered or made available for public sale," said Malcolm, pausing to take a deep breath. "It's valued at one and a half million dollars!"

Marcus's eyes widened involuntarily as he listened to the words seeming to fall from Mr. Abernathy's lips in ultra-slow motion. As he opened his mouth to speak, Malcolm once again raised a finger, cutting Marcus off.

"The penny your father concealed inside the watch case for you... It's worth over *two* million dollars!" said Malcolm.

Marcus's mouth suddenly felt as if he'd been eating cotton balls. Raising the glass of cognac to his lips with a trembling hand, he slammed it down, unable to produce a single intelligent word as his mind seemed to melt down inside his very skull.

"Are you serious?!" asked Marcus, incredulously.

"Deadly so," replied Malcolm. "You sir, have shown me the two rarest and most valuable items I have ever had the honor of holding in my hands."

Rushing across the shop to the front door, he locked it and pulled the shades, saying "We need to get these to a bank safe deposit box immediately."

"My bank is less than a hundred yards from here, two doors down from your shop!" said Marcus, excitedly.

"Okay. You take them there right now!" said Mr. Abernathy. "And, whatever you do, don't mention to anyone; even at the bank, what exactly you're putting inside that safe deposit box. I'll call a bonded auction house in Boise, and see if they can send someone over for them as soon as possible... That is, if you would like to sell them," he added.

"Okay," said Marcus, peeking out the shop window and looking in both directions before opening the door and nearly running to his bank only a few steps further down the sidewalk. A few minutes later, he returned after having secured both items in the safe deposit box inside the bank's main vault.

Within an hour, a representative from the auction house arrived at Mr. Abernathy's shop door. He was carrying a briefcase containing enough cash to purchase both items outright, circumventing the need for Marcus to wait until the next auction. After an hour of deliberation, Marcus decided to only sell the penny; unable to part with his father's pocket watch at any price.

Accompanying Marcus to the bank, the bonded auction house representative from Boise completed the purchase transaction which was officially notarized by the bank manager before taking possession of the penny. Fifteen minutes later, Marcus left the bank after having completely paid off his mortgage and deposited all but one hundred thousand dollars of the remaining cash into his account.

It was only 3:00 p.m. when Marcus returned to Mr. Abernathy's shop. While Malcolm insisted that a hundred thousand dollars was far too much to take for the role he'd played, the two men were finally able to agree on a commission of fifty-thousand dollars.

"Thank you, Mr. Abernathy," said Marcus. "You are an incredible man, and I can't thank you enough for everything you've done for me."

"It's been a pleasure, Sir," stated Mr. Abernathy. "I'd wish you good luck, but you've had plenty of that today."

Nodding, Marcus smiled and exited the shop, only to reappear a few seconds later. "I forgot to pay for the watch repair," he said, placing the remaining fifty thousand in cash on the countertop. "This should cover it!" he added, scurrying out the door before Mr. Abernathy could object.

As the day drew to an end, Malcolm had to smile as he considered the events of the past few hours. Tugging at the chain dangling from his pocket and connected to the third button from the bottom of his vest, he checked the time on his pocket watch to confirm it was closing time.

Looking down at the timepiece, he decided to clean and polish his Rolex® Rattrapante before leaving for the day. Who knows...? Perhaps after a proper buffing, his might look just as amazing as Marcus's.

Chapter Four

"When did I get so old?" thought Beatrice, looking at her reflection in the bathroom mirror. It seemed to her, like only yesterday that she was either hiking, boating, or exploring some unknown corner of the world, purely for the sake of saying she'd been there.

Lately, it was an adventure just to make it out to the mailbox and back. Had it not been for her nephew, who'd moved in with her after graduating from high school, she wouldn't have even been able to manage the upkeep on her home. In fact, she'd actually considered moving into a small condo at a nearby retirement community before Nathan arrived.

While his work hours were somewhat odd, he did pay all of the utilities and helped her out with the groceries each week. At first, he seemed to be a blessing in disguise but lately, the disguise seemed much more prevalent than the blessing.

It was an old house, and after years of providing shelter for her and her late husband, along with four children who were all grown and living with their own families spread across the country now, it could use some tender love and care. While Beatrice was more than capable of fixing cabinet hinges, replacing electrical sockets, and repairing worn out odds and ends, when the refrigerator suddenly stopped cooling, she needed someone competent to take a look at it.

Time and again, she'd asked Nathan to call someone, but he never seemed to find the time. Finally, after tossing out another perfectly good head of lettuce, Beatrice decided to take matters into her own hands.

As if on cue, she noticed the flyer on the dining room table next to the stack of mail dropped there by Nathan. Perhaps the name of the shop imprinted on the flyer had reminded him to call someone. He could have left it there, intending to contact them when he woke up later that afternoon.

Beatrice decided it was something she'd handle herself. It had been awhile since a new business had opened in downtown Mountain Home, and she was curious to take a peek inside. Grabbing the flyer and her car keys, she headed out the door actually excited about doing something to break the monotony of her otherwise hum drum daily routine.

A few minutes later, she was parked out front of Mr. Abernathy's shop with the flyer clutched in her hand. As she approached, in typical Malcolm Abernathy style, he was there to open the door for her.

"Good afternoon, Ma'am," he said with a smile. "What can I fix for you today?"

"My oh my!" exclaimed Beatrice. "This place is amazing! Do you mind if I look around for a moment?"

"By all means!" said Malcolm with a smile.

She wandered through the store in sheer delight, recalling cherished memories with so many of the items she recognized from her childhood. From manual mixers to the peddle operated sewing machine, being inside the shop was like stepping into a time capsule filled with her own personal memorabilia.

After nearly an hour of wandering aimlessly through the aisles, she turned the find Malcolm standing behind her smiling.

"It's a lot to take in at once, don't you think?" he said. "Even I get lost, back in those racks once in a while,"

"You could charge admission here if you wanted to," said Beatrice. "I'd be a regular visitor, even if you did."

"You are welcome to come by as often as you'd like," said Malcolm. "I certainly enjoy an appreciative eye."

"Well, I actually came by to ask if you make house calls. I have a refrigerator that just doesn't seem to cool anymore, and I was hoping you could perhaps take a look at it. I'd have brought it here myself, but the backseats of modern-day sedans aren't what they used to be."

"I suppose I'd be up for a lunchtime fieldtrip," said Malcolm. "I can take a few tools with me and have a look at it. Maybe I can fix it right away, and if not, I can at least get a bead on the problem and come back tomorrow."

"Now, that sounds like a reasonable plan to me," said Beatrice. "My house is out on Old Tollgate Road, and since the road ends at my property, just keep driving until there's nowhere else to go. I'll have a fresh pot of coffee and a slice of my Dutch apple pie waiting for you."

"Well, who could resist a slice of Dutch apple pie?" said Malcolm with a smile. "I'll lock up here and head over in a few minutes."

When he arrived, she was sitting on the porch steps waiting. After he parked, she walked towards him and extended her hand, saying "Welcome to Villa Fantastico!"

Reaching out and shaking her hand, he said "Thanks for the invitation. I haven't been in town for very long and this is my first house call."

"Well, it's not official until you've had some coffee and a slice or two of that pie, I was telling you about," said Beatrice.

Inside the house, Beatrice had already set the small table in the kitchen for her lunch guest. There were ham and cheese sandwiches made with home-baked bread, along with a cup for the freshly brewed coffee, just finishing up in the coffee maker on the countertop.

"Since it's a working lunch, I figured we should probably get you fed first. The refrigerator isn't going anywhere," Beatrice said with a smile.

As they sat together enjoying lunch and exchanging a bit of their personal backgrounds with one another, Malcolm was already analyzing the peculiar sounds coming from the refrigerator. The compressor was coming on far too often as it tried to cool the appliance's interior. By the time he'd finished the enormous slice of mouthwateringly delicious apple pie, he'd pretty much diagnosed the problem and was ready to get to work on it.

"When was the last time you swept behind the refrigerator?" Malcolm asked.

"Um... Never," said Beatrice, sheepishly. "That thing hasn't been moved in twenty-five years. It's probably glued to the floor by now," she admitted.

Sliding a long nylon towing belt over and behind the refrigerator, he slipped it around his waist and leaned back. Expecting serious resistance, he was surprised when it easily glided towards him with just a gentle tug.

"Twenty-five years, you said?" queried Malcolm, curiously furrowing his forehead. "That is highly unlikely."

After pulling the refrigerator clear of the wall and cabinets surrounding it, he got down on the floor and reached into the compressor cavity underneath it. "There's something down here blocking the airflow around the condenser fan. I think it's causing the compressor to overheat and shut down before it can circulate the cold air which cools the inside.

Grabbing onto what felt like a travel bag, he pulled it out of the compressor cavity. Sure enough, it was a backpack similar to those carried by students for their books and school supplies. Placing it on the table, he invited Beatrice to open it and take a look inside.

When she opened the backpack, the color drained from her face, and her cheerful demeanor evaporated into thin air. Looking up at Mr. Abernathy, she slowly slid the backpack over to him. After looking inside, he quickly closed it, removed it from the table, and placed it back underneath the refrigerator before pushing it back against the wall just as he'd discovered it.

Speaking quietly, he leaned in close to her, saying "You are in danger, Beatrice. You need to get out of here... now!"

"Where am I supposed to go?" she asked. "This is my home! Why do *I* need to leave?"

"Leave where, Auntie Bea?" came a voice from the kitchen doorway. "Why would you need to leave?" asked Nathan, looking curiously at Mr. Abernathy.

"Oh, Nathan. I... I was just telling Mr. Abernathy, here..."

"There could be a radon gas leak beneath the house," said Malcolm, rescuing Beatrice from the awkward situation. "You may want to get away for a few days, until you can get someone out here to look into it."

Nodding, Nathan said "Sure Auntie Bea. You can take a trip to Boise and I'll set you up there anywhere you'd like."

Looking up at Nathan, then to Malcolm, and back to Nathan again, Beatrice said "I couldn't let you do that Nathan. Warehouse jobs don't pay that kind of money, and who knows how long it would take to get someone from Elmore County in here to inspect everything?"

"Don't worry about it," said Nathan. "I've got some overtime pay coming, and it'll more than cover a little Boise vacation."

"I have a testing device somewhere in my shop," said Malcolm. "I can come out tomorrow morning and check out all of the cabinets, behind the washer and dryer, and pull the refrigerator out and check out everything back there too. I'll need you to come over to my store to submit the work order though." Looking at Beatrice, he asked "Do you think you could drop by sometime before 5:00 p.m. today?"

"Sure, Mr. Abernathy," replied Beatrice. "I could swing by in an hour, or so if that works for you."

"That would be perfect," replied Malcolm, grabbing his tool bag, and walking casually toward the front door.

Nathan and Beatrice followed Malcolm to the front porch, where he turned and said, "One more thing... I will need you to bring another slice of that amazing apple pie with you." With a smile, he added "Two slices if you'd like to bring Nathan along."

"Nah," said Nathan. "I have to get some rest before I go to work tonight. I'll check it out another time."

"As you wish," said Malcolm. "You don't know what you're missing."

With a tip of his hat, he got into his car and headed back up Old Tollgate Road toward town. His heart was pounding like a drum, despite the cool exterior he'd displayed before leaving Beatrice's house. Once inside the shop, he was pacing nervously back and forth looking out the store window every few seconds, wondering what was taking Beatrice so long. Finally, after what seemed an eternity she pulled up in front of the shop and quickly walked inside.

"Oh my god!" she exclaimed. "Was that what I *think* it was?"

"If you're thinking it was several hundred thousand dollars' worth of cocaine and a couple hundred grand in cash, then yes! It's exactly what you think it was!"

"What are we going to do?" asked Beatrice, frantically. "I need that stuff out of my house right now, and I'm not going back there until it's gone!"

"Listen," said Malcolm. "Having you come here, gives him time to get that crap out of your house. After telling him I'd be coming by in the morning to inspect everything, you can be sure, the entire house will be clean as a whistle by the time I get there."

"Another thing," he added. "you need to stay somewhere else tonight, and make sure Nathan does not know where that somewhere is. I have a friend at City Hall who I can ask to help out with the radon inspection. In order to keep you safe, it needs to appear legit, in case he's watching."

After speaking with Amanda Witherspoon at City Hall, she was happy to assist, and within minutes, she called back to confirm an appointment for the radon gas inspection. In the meantime, Beatrice had reserved a hotel room and was already on her way to Boise.

A few minutes before closing time, Malcolm saw a pickup pull into a parking spot in front of his shop. It was Nathan.

Even though it was nearly time to lock up the shop, Malcolm, in his typical courteous manner, met Nathan at the door with a smile, saying "Nathan. What can I fix for you today?"

As he came through the door, Nathan was clearly scanning the shop for other people, and apparently looking for security cameras.

"Your aunt isn't here, Nathan. Actually, I'm quite surprised to see you here as well," said Malcolm after not receiving a response to his traditional greeting. "What brings you in this late?"

"So, where did she go?" asked Nathan. "She never came back to the house or mentioned whether or not she'd be staying in Boise tonight."

"That's not something I can help you with, young man. She was only here long enough to complete the work order, then shortly afterwards, she left," said Malcolm. "She's been gone for hours."

"Show me the work order," said Nathan, staring unblinkingly at Malcolm.

Without so much as a moment of hesitation, Malcolm turned and picked up the clipboard still lying on the reception counter near the front door and handed it to Nathan. It was clearly a work order for the radon inspection at his aunt's address, with a confirmation number from the clerk at City Hall.

Skeptically reviewing the work order, Nathan asked "Why did you come out there in the first place? Auntie Bea's pie is good, but I'm not sure it would have been worth closing up your business for."

"The refrigerator isn't cooling, and she wanted me to take a look at it," said Malcolm. "While we were eating lunch, I was able to diagnose the problem without even needing to unplug it."

"Oh really?" said Nathan, before asking "So, why didn't you fix it?"

"I couldn't," replied Malcolm. "It's the condenser fan, and I didn't have one with me, so there was no need to even bother. I'll take one with me in the morning and switch them out while the county is performing the radon inspection," he added, looking down at his watch. "Now, if you'll excuse me, it's time for me to close up shop, and I have a terribly impatient Pomeranian waiting for me to come home and feed her."

As he escorted his last customer towards the front door, Nathan stopped and turned to face Malcolm. "Listen, Mister Abernathy... I don't trust you, and I don't like you coming out to the house snooping around. From now on, if you need to come to the house for anything, you're going to have to clear it with me first." Stepping well inside Malcolm's personal space, he added, "Have I made myself clear?"

"Well, what you've made abundantly clear is that you're hiding some sort of unseemly activity in your aunt's house, and you're afraid I'll discover it and tell her about it," said Malcolm. "Based on your presence here and your overall degree of paranoia, I'd say you're afraid I already have."

Visibly irritated, Nathan snapped saying "Listen, old man..."

"No, *you* listen!" interrupted Malcolm. "Pushing around and disrespecting Beatrice in her own home might work for you out on Old Tollgate Road, but I can assure you; It would be much less beneficial for you here, in my establishment. I'd suggest you get *your* affairs together before the Environmental Safety Inspector shows up at *her* house in the morning, and I'd highly recommend you take two steps backwards immediately so that I can close the front door of my shop."

Begrudgingly, Nathan did back out the door which immediately closed, only an inch or so shy of his nose. As he continued to stare through the shop window, Malcolm pulled the shade down and walked away, ignoring him completely.

Nathan stood there fuming for a full minute before realizing he looked like a fool, staring at a lowered window shade. Obviously unaccustomed to being rebuffed and rejected, Nathan was at a loss for words, and a few seconds later, he was angrily peeling out of the parking lot.

What you'd think everyone who ever lived near a military installation would know, is that first; if you're going to speed through town on Main Street, never ever do it at 5:00 p.m. on a weekday. That's when the workday ends for most military personnel, and local police are just itching to pull someone over as they leave the installation. Next; if you do speed, at least be very courteous to the police officer who will invariably stop you before you've even gone a mile. Finally, if you are going to speed *and* be disrespectful to the police officer, make sure you're not carrying a backpack full of cocaine and drug money underneath the passenger seat beside you!

Needless to say, Nathan missed all three swings during his turn at bat, striking out miserably. Of course, it didn't help that earlier, someone had also called in Nathan's plate number for suspicion of trafficking illicit or controlled substances.

The next day, headlines which would probably have covered the rattlesnake captured by Mountain Home Animal Control in a convenience store parking lot, were bumped by the story touting the largest drug bust in Mountain Home history!

When Malcolm showed up at Beatrice's place with the Environmental Safety Inspector, he was somewhat surprised to see her property was swarming with local and federal law enforcement agents who, after searching her entire property found nothing connecting Beatrice to her nephew's arrest for drug possession with the intent to distribute.

The raid had been conducted at 6:00 a.m. sharp, while Beatrice slept soundly in her room at The Riverside Hotel in Boise. Presenting the work order, she'd completed for the radon inspection; they were allowed entry into the residence just as the agents were wrapping up their property search and preparing to leave.

In the kitchen, Malcolm went directly to the refrigerator, opening the door and sticking his arm inside to check the temperature.

It was as cold as ice.

Chapter Five

Most things that break are not that difficult to analyze and repair if you understand the principles upon which they are based. The majority of man-made things are either manual, chemical, mechanical, or electrical, so if you can identify their fundamental basis, you can trace the reason for their malfunction back to the roots upon which they were built.

Regardless of their origin, most man-made products were created to make a specific job easier, allowing one person to perform tasks which would otherwise require either additional time or manpower to accomplish. If you know what something was created for, you can better understand what it should do, that it's not doing.

While most devices are simple to understand and fix, the people who wield them are infinitely more difficult to analyze and comprehend. It also bears consideration that some broken things... should stay that way.

James Calderone, like many other residents, was a veteran who had been assigned to Mountain Home Air Force Base earlier in his career. He'd fallen in love with Idaho's great outdoors and couldn't wait to retire and move there permanently. While he certainly enjoyed the hunting and fishing opportunities Idaho afforded him, the proximity of the military installation had been a major factor in his final decision.

As a former Air Force pilot, he loved looking up as military fighter aircraft streaked across the wide-open skies overhead. Even though his property was directly in the flight path of the base, the sound was more soothing to him than annoying, and he never regretted purchasing the land that almost no one else would ever have wanted.

While his new domicile had good "bones", it was still an old house, and old houses commonly have things about them which have fallen into disrepair. The previous owner had lived there for over forty years, and after he died none of his children were willing to put in the work required to renovate the place, just so they could be plagued by aircraft noise night and day.

James bought the house for under fifty thousand dollars, paying cash for it almost on the spot. Since he was retired, it would give him a long-term project to work on, without it morphing into something overwhelming. Besides, after clocking out for the last time after nearly thirty years of military service, he was looking forward to taking life at a snail's pace.

His first home project was stripping and resealing the hardwood floors in the three bedrooms and the hallway. Once the floors were done, he repainted the walls of each bedroom in different colors, while sticking with classic matte white for the hallway. Since his furniture hadn't yet arrived from Nellis Air Force Base, where he had retired, he purchased a folding cot from a camping supply store along with a card table and two folding chairs for the kitchen.

One benefit of living a little off the beaten path, was the abundance of wildlife inhabiting the area around James's house. Each morning, he'd sit by the back door in the kitchen watching everything from rabbits and prairie dogs, to the foxes and coyotes which hunted them. Although he never really knew which animals would parade past his property every morning, he enjoyed them all without any sort of personal attachment to any of them.

Eventually, he'd need to repair the double-rail fence out at the edge of his property. While he was in no hurry to get to it, being directly in his field of view when looking out the kitchen window, it was a bit of an eyesore. Once he was done with the remaining indoor renovations, he'd get to work clearing out and repairing things around the property outside. However, for now, he was content just watching the parade of wildlife each morning while having his first cup of coffee.

A month after moving in, he was sitting in the kitchen just before dawn having breakfast when he discovered he had new visitors. Just beyond the fence, he noticed five horses there in the tall yellow grass. One of them was staring right at him, and while he was only speculating, to James it appeared he was standing guard while the other horses grazed in carefree serenity.

With his curiosity getting the better of him, he opened the sliding glass door leading from the kitchen out onto the patio. Four of the five horses bolted at the unexpected sound, but the large black stallion remained, continuing to stare at James until the sound of the other horses faded over the hill to safety behind him. After a final glance, the horse lifted his head as if to say, "see you later", and gallantly trotted off in the direction of the others.

Throughout the day, James found his thoughts circling around the stallion as he installed ceramic tile on the kitchen floor, and along the backsplash wall behind the stove. That evening as he cleaned his tools out on the patio, he saw the small band of horses off in the distance with the stallion silhouetted against the evening sky at the top of the hill.

Calling it quits for the day, he hopped in his truck and headed over to the base to pick up a few things from the commissary. When he passed the produce department, on a whim, he picked up a case of apples, wondering if he could entice the wild horses to come closer. Even though he had no intention of ever riding them, he did feel a sort of kinship with them, and hoped they would stick around for a while. Since he didn't yet have a refrigerator or freezer, he left the case of apples outside in a shaded corner of the patio.

The next day, the moving van arrived with his household goods from Nevada. Once everything was in its proper place, his hard work preparing the house was impressively obvious. While there were still small things which needed attention, for the most part he'd transformed the ugly duckling house into a beautiful swan he could certainly be proud of.

In the weeks that followed, James looked into the possibility of formally adopting the wild horses and caring for them. He discovered that the Idaho Bureau of Land Management actually had an adoption program in place; however, it strictly prohibited private citizens from luring in and feeding wild horses or attempting to capture and domesticate them.

    Thinking better of it, he decided that some things were meant to be left as they are. After all, the beauty of wild horses is their absolute freedom, and their desire to be near his property without James's external influence, made him appreciate their regular morning visits even more.

    The water in James's house came from a well on his property. Even though the water pressure at the faucets left much to be desired, it was clean and crystal clear and tasted better than any other water he'd ever drank. One morning as he was just rinsing off in the shower, the water pressure dropped to an even weaker drizzle, and he could hear clicking sounds inside the walls coming from the pipes. A few seconds later... silence.

    Water pumps are built to function flawlessly for years on end, but when they go, it's usually and unexpected surprise of the not-so-welcome variety. Of course, James's first thought was to have the entire thing replaced with a brand-new assembly and pump, and some people would have taken that route just to avoid getting their hands dirty. James however, upon hearing the price for the job was approaching three-thousand dollars, he decided to take a stab at the repair himself.

It took him several hours and a lot of creativity, just to get the pump out of the ground. In the end, he built a simple pully system incorporating the wheels from a rusted tiller he found in the shed, and nearly the entire two-hundred feet of cable on his truck winch to extract it from the well casing.

Stretched out across the ground, the pump assembly looked like some giant conquered serpent over which he now triumphantly stood. After inspecting the entire length of it for pipe damage and possible breaks in the power cables, he determined the problem was indeed the motor and pump assembly which would need to be either repaired or replaced.

James had already made several trips into Mountain Home during the renovation process to purchase supplies and specialized tools for various projects. While he was sure he could find a new pump assembly at a local hardware store, the intriguing sign over the door of Mr. Abernathy's shop caught his attention while waiting at the intersection for the light to change.

He decided to drop in and at least ask about repairing the old well pump before spending nearly a grand for a new one. After backing into the parking spot in front of the entrance, he dropped the tailgate and grabbed the pump assembly. When he turned around, he was greeted by a smiling Mr. Abernathy.

"Good afternoon, Sir," Malcolm said almost musically, with the usual accompanying smile. "What can I fix for you today?"

"Good afternoon to you!" responded James, also smiling. "My name's James and I was headed down the street to the hardware store when I noticed your sign from the intersection over there. I figured that since your shop is right along the way, I may as well stop and see if you could repair my old well pump before I buy a new one."

"Excellent!" said Malcolm, holding the door open for James as he entered the shop. Taking the pump assembly from him, he said "My name's Malcolm. Have a seat and let's take a quick look."

Malcolm worked very quickly, and in just a few minutes he had the assembly broken down into its two primary elements: the pump and the motor. Since the pump element seemed to be in fairly good shape and would still spin freely inside the stainless-steel enclosure, Malcolm turned his attention to the motor, discovering it had seized.

"Here's your problem, Sir," said Malcolm, showing James how tightly that part of the assembly had locked up. "The motor is supposed to drive the pump elements that move the water upward into the reservoir. This one isn't turning at all," he said, tapping on the housing with a screwdriver.

"How much would it cost to fix or replace it?" asked James.

"If you can leave it with me for about two hours, I can break it down and see what's jamming it up," said

Malcolm. "These things are meant to last up to forty years, and this one is only about half that age judging by the model and serial numbers."

"That would be great. Even if you can't fix it, it'll save me a couple hundred bucks if I only need to replace the motor."

"Then, if you have any errands to run here in town, you can swing back by around 4:30 p.m. and I should either have it fixed or at least narrowed down enough for you to decide how you'd like to proceed."

"Sounds good," said James. "I'll see you at 4:30 p.m."

While James was gone, Malcolm completely disassembled the motor and thoroughly cleaned every single part inside. It didn't take long for him to discover the bearings were worn and needed to be replaced. Apparently one of them had been faulty when assembled at the factory, which prevented the shaft from spinning smoothly and remaining in alignment. With the majority of the motor's load being born by the one working bearing, the shaft couldn't rotate freely. Eventually, the defective bearing disintegrated completely, and the added resistance caused the motor's internal circuit breaker to pop.

After cleaning and polishing the motor's drive shaft and replacing the worn bearings, he reset the internal circuit breaker and reassembled everything, making sure all of the seals were watertight. When he powered it up again, the motor ran smoother than ever, and by the time James returned, Mr. Abernathy had the entire assembly cleaned and ready to go.

"Wow!" said James. "This thing looks brand-new!"

"Wait until you get it reconnected and back down in the well," said Malcolm. "You should notice a significant increase in your water pressure, and the whole thing should last you at least another twenty or thirty years," he concluded.

"Now, that's what I call outstanding customer service," said James. "How much do I owe you?"

"One-hundred-fifty dollars for everything, including all parts and labor," replied Mr. Abernathy. "If it gives you any trouble over the next ten or twenty years, bring it back and I'll fix it again for you."

"Thank you!" said James, leaving the cash on the reception counter. "I have a feeling we will be seeing a lot of one another over the next few months," he added.

"Well, if you ever need anything repaired, you know where you can find me," Malcolm replied.

By nightfall, James had the pump back inside the well with everything reconnected and running smoothly. Sure enough, the water pressure was noticeably better at every faucet in the house. Proud of the work he'd done for the day, he cracked open a beer and took a seat outside on the patio where he'd moved the card table and folding chairs after his furniture had been delivered.

Looking over towards the covered corner of the patio, James noticed a few of the apples seemed to be missing from the wooden crate he'd placed there. He smiled to himself while sipping his beer, wondering which of his new four-legged friends had paid him a visit while he was in town earlier that day.

The reveal came shortly before dawn the very next morning when James entered the kitchen. Peering out through the window, he saw the stallion was in his backyard just inside the fence! While his heart was doing somersaults, James's demeanor remained calm as he prepared a pot of coffee.

Shortly after 6:00 a.m., he opened the sliding glass door leading out to the patio. This time, neither the four horses just beyond the fence nor the stallion inside it bolted, and they continued grazing when James took a seat outside at the card table to drink his morning coffee. James also noted that the case of apples he'd moved to the far edge of the patio was running perilously low. He'd have to pick up another case at the commissary on his next trip to the airbase.

Just before dawn, the stallion trotted back through the opening in the broken fence and with a final glance back at the house, he and the other horses vanished out of sight as sunlight broke over the ridge. During the middle of the day, the horses never grazed openly in the field, preferring to come out of their hiding spot either early in the morning, or late evenings after the sun had sunk behind the hills to the west.

After completing the interior renovations, James began cleaning up the property surrounding the house. While doing so, he discovered there was a disconnected sprinkler system installed around the property as well. It had probably remained unused because the defective pump couldn't provide enough pressure to effectively push water through the irrigation system. Now that the pump was running at full efficiency, it could easily cover his entire backyard *and* throw water halfway across the field beyond the fence along his property line.

After months spent getting his house and property into tip-top shape, James was curious to see what lay beyond the hill he had affectionately dubbed "Stallion Ridge" behind his property. Hiking out to it, he was shocked to see just how steep and rocky the embankment was on the other side. There was a small creek running through the narrow ravine below, which probably explained why the horses preferred spending the hottest part of the day there. There were also numerous stone overhangs that provided shade at different points along the creek, which would certainly be welcome shelters to a band of horses looking to escape the midday sun.

After a while spent peering over the edge, he concluded that weaving his way down to the bottom of the ravine would be a fool's errand, or at least, an adventure for another time. Why go searching for something that comes to you twice, every single day?

As time passed, the pre-dawn and dusk visitations became a regular part of James's day. Even though, they weren't officially *his* horses, he named them all. The stallion was, Sampson, the darkest of the four mares was Silhouette, the honey-colored one was called Honey (go figure), the brown mare with the white splash extending from just over her eyes to her crown was called Princess, and the smallest of the four mares, he named Baby Doll.

Unless James was alone at the house, the horses would never approach, although his visitors could clearly hear them running along the ridge in the distance. Obviously, James had gained their trust over time, and it was something he vowed never to betray. He loved them and they knew it.

As autumn drew to a close, he became concerned that perhaps they wouldn't be able to find enough food to sustain them through the winter. Concerned for them, he drove into town and stopped at a feed company to have a few bales of hay delivered to his property. At the checkout line, he ran into Mr. Abernathy, who's shop had become a regular stop on nearly all of his trips into town.

"Hello James!" said Malcolm, genuinely happy to see him.

"Hey Malcolm!" replied James excitedly. "I stopped by your shop, but the sign said you were out to lunch."

"Yes. It probably should have said I was out to lunch for Coco," said Malcolm. "Since I started feeding her dog food from here, she turns her nose up at everything else. I'm not sure what they put in this stuff, but Coco literally loves it!".

"Well, hopefully their hay and horse feed are just as irresistible," said James with a smile.

"Thinking of getting some horses?" asked Malcolm.

"Not really," said James. "but I do have a small band of wild horses who wander up to my place from one of the herd management areas. The folks from the BLM never come out to check on them, so I thought I would store some hay and feed at my place for them, just in case this winter comes in as hard as the Farmer's Almanac is predicting for this year."

"Where is your place, again?" asked the feed store manager.

"I bought the old Todd place about half-an-hour's drive from here," said James.

Looking up, the store manager said, "There aren't any wild horses out that way. In fact, there haven't been any horses out there since the Soda Fire a few years back. The BLM rounded them all up and moved them out of the fire's path to a safer area."

"Well, they must have missed a few," said James. "Because, I've had a group of them out near my place every day since I moved into it back in late summer."

Resting his elbows on the countertop, the manager tilted his ballcap back before saying, "Mister, I was out there with the folks from the BLM when we rounded all of them up. We swept that entire area clean after the fire reached the creek behind Old Man Todd's property. We were able to save most of them, but we lost five at that creek when the fire forced them up against the side of the ravine. We tried, but we just couldn't get to them in time, and they didn't have anywhere to go."

"Really?" said James with a look of utter shock on his face. "Are you sure they didn't get out somehow?"

"We all hoped and prayed that they would," said the man. "but with the fire spreading through that gap so fast, all we could do is listen to them die. A stallion and four mares... It was horrible."

James's face turned ashen as the man continued, "Old Man Todd must have bought and borrowed every inch of garden hose in town, trying to keep the flames back until we could figure out how to rescue them somehow. Unfortunately, his old well pump couldn't generate enough pressure to put more than a sprinkle on them, and with every fire station in three states deployed to battle the fire, there was no one else to call. Still, he stayed right there with them until the smoke got him too. He was still holding onto the hose when they found his body."

Without a word, James turned and left the store. He was nearly in a trance when he pulled up in front of his place, then got out of his truck and walked around to the back of the house. At the edge of his property, he stopped at the opening in the rail fence, taking a closer look.

It was clear to see the fence had been knocked down from inside his property; probably by Old Man Todd himself. Wresting the dangling rails away from the fence, he dragged them back up to the house and propped them against the shed. He'd use them as firewood during the coming winter.

When the sun dropped below the hills to the west, James took a seat at the card table on his patio. As usual, his visitors were right on time, with the four mares grazing outside the fence while Sampson stood watch over them from James's backyard. They remained there with him until the gray evening sky faded to a pitch-black canvas for the stars above, before heading back over the hill to the creek beyond.

Watching them disappear into the night, James said "Goodnight, my friends. I'll see you in the morning." Smiling as he turned to walk back inside, he added "I'll leave the gate open for you."

Chapter Six

In the few short months after Mr. Abernathy opened his shop, he'd become a popular figure in the Mountain Home community, if a rather peculiar one. The word of his talent and ability to fix nearly anything had quickly spread throughout the relatively small town, and the volume of his business had increased substantially.

One brisk autumn day as he sat at his workbench repairing a German Cuckoo clock, Mr. Abernathy noticed a young boy spying on him through the shop window. It wasn't the first time he'd seen the young man, and it was obvious he was curious about what went on inside the mysterious little shop.

Acting as if he needed something to finish the repair, Malcolm disappeared into his office and left the building through the side door. Quietly, he crept up behind the boy as he peered through the window with his hands cupped around his eyes for better visibility. When he was only a few inches away, Malcolm bent down and cupped his hands around his eyes as he peeked through the window as well, saying "You can't see much from here."

The boy was frozen with indecision, not knowing whether to run or just stand there with his eyes and mouth wide open. Finally, he backed away and turned, preparing to run off.

"You know..." said Malcolm. "It's much warmer inside, and you can see much better from in there, than you can from out here through this dirty window."

After a few steps when he realized he wasn't being chased away, he turned and looked back at the unusually dressed man with the waxed moustache.

"I'm not going to bite you," said Malcolm with a smile. "In fact, I was wondering if you'd like a job. I have a few things around here that I could really use some help with."

"My mom says you're probably a warlock, and that I shouldn't come around your shop," said the boy, obviously conflicted.

"So why didn't you listen to your mother?" asked Malcolm, adding "You should always obey your parents."

"I finished all of my homework, and I got bored," said the boy. "She's asleep now, and I'll be back home before she wakes up anyway."

"Okay then, here's what I'd like you to do," said Malcolm, writing something inside his pocket notepad with a pencil, and handing it to the boy. "My name is Mr. Abernathy, and this is the address and phone number to my shop. I'd like you to tell your mom I've offered you a job cleaning up around here after school. It'll only be a couple of hours each day, and I'll pay you ten dollars per hour."

"Ten dollars!?" asked the boy excitedly.

"Yes, but one of your parents will need to come by with you before I can officially hire you," said Malcolm.

"It's only my mom and me," said the boy. "But she doesn't like to leave the house much anymore." Looking down at the sidewalk, he continued. "She caught something called PTSD when she was working over in Afghanistan. I don't really know what that is, but when she came back home, my dad said he couldn't take it anymore, so he left."

"Well, I am deeply sorry to hear that," said Malcolm before asking "What's your name, young man?".

"My name is Michael Anderson, but you can call me Mikey. All my friends call me Mikey," said the boy.

"Well, Mikey," said Malcolm with a smile. "Please give the note to your mother, and have her contact me whenever she's ready, okay?"

"Okay," said the boy, as he headed down the sidewalk and disappeared around the corner.

Later that afternoon, the phone rang, and Malcolm answered it to find it was Mikey's mother on the line. "This is Heidi Anderson," she said. "I'd like to speak with Malcolm Abernathy."

"Speaking," said Malcolm, adding "Thank you for calling. It's a pleasure to speak with you."

"Thank you, Mr. Abernathy," she said. "Mikey told me you needed someone to help clean up around your place, and that you offered him a job. Is that true?"

"I did, indeed," answered Malcolm. "He seems like a nice young man, and I could certainly use the help. Do you think you could come by with him tomorrow after school? That way we can make it official."

For a moment, there was silence on the other end of the line; however, Malcolm allowed the silence to continue until Mrs. Anderson was ready to speak.

"It's just that Mikey can get a little carried away at times, and he stretches the truth once in a while," she said. "He certainly does need something to keep him busy after school though. Otherwise, he ends up getting into mischief and starts acting out."

"Yes ma'am. That's exactly what young boys do. I was one, myself many years ago... if you can believe that," said Malcolm with an audible chuckle.

"I'd like to come by," said Mrs. Anderson. "but I have trouble getting out the door sometimes, due to the medicine my doctor has me taking. It's hard for me to keep appointments *and* promises, so I hope you won't hold it against Mikey if I have trouble making it over to see you."

Malcolm could clearly sense the distress in her voice as she softly spoke into the phone. Post-traumatic stress disorder can manifest itself in so many different ways, making it difficult for those dealing with it to cope in strange or new environments. With the thousands of objects and oddities inside Malcolm's shop, the possibility of them triggering an anxiety attack was something he found unnecessary and avoidable.

"If you'd like, we can complete most of the application over the phone, and I can bring it by to meet you personally and get your signature when I close up the shop today," Malcolm offered.

"Would you actually do that?" asked Mrs. Anderson, apparently surprised.

75

"Of course," said Malcolm, adding "It's no trouble for me at all."

Together, they completed Mikey's employment application, and after closing up for the day, Malcolm headed over to the address on the form. It was literally within three minute's walking distance from his shop. After knocking, he waited patiently outside the door.

A few seconds later, Heidi slightly opened the door while cautiously looking through the crack at Malcolm. "Mr. Abernathy?" she asked.

"Yes ma'am," said Malcolm, holding up the application they'd completed together earlier.

Timidly reaching through the narrow opening, she took the papers and closed the door. Malcolm waited patiently outside the door while she signed the documents inside and handed them back to him through the same narrow crack.

"Thank you!" said Malcolm. "Mikey is going to be a tremendous help to me, and you should feel free to come by at any time to check out the environment he'll be working in."

As he turned to leave, from behind the door, he heard her ask, "Can you stay for a moment? I mean... can we talk for just a minute while you wait outside the door?"

Understanding how awkward this must be for *her*, he said "Of course," before sliding down onto the floor beside her door and leaning back against the wall.

"It's been over a month since I've set foot outside this door, Mr. Abernathy. I know it probably sounds unreasonable to most people, but... I'm afraid," said Heidi as they both sat back-to-back on opposite sides of the same wall. "Mikey is a great kid, and it tortures me that I keep him trapped in here most of the time because I'm so afraid of what's out there lying in wait for me."

"No need to explain yourself to me, Mrs. Anderson," Malcolm said. "We all have our own battles to fight, and our own victories to celebrate. I respect that, and I would never judge you or Mikey for the way you choose to heal. You can rest assured he'll be safe and in good hands working for me."

"Promise?" asked Mrs. Anderson. "He's all I have left."

"I promise," said Malcolm.

He could hear the two of them discussing the pros and cons before she finally answered, saying "Okay. He will be there right after school tomorrow at around 3:00 p.m. if that works for you."

Rising to his feet again, Malcolm said "That would be perfect, and I will walk home with him after we close at 5:00 p.m."

"Thank you, Mr. Abernathy... for everything," said Heidi.

"Have a wonderful evening, Mrs. Anderson," said Malcolm before heading back to his car in the parking lot behind the shop and driving home.

Mikey showed up at the shop shortly before 3:00 p.m. at which time he was outfitted with an apron and a broom. He'd been thinking about it the entire day and was incredibly excited. He'd never even been inside the shop and now he had a job there... his very first job, at that!

Mikey proved to be a diligent worker, and eager to please Mr. Abernathy. In the two hours of his very first workday, he'd swept the floors and wiped down all the countertops including Malcolm's workbench. Afterwards, he went outside and cleaned all of the fingerprints and smudges from the windows; the majority of them being his own.

He was still working at dusting the different items on the shelves when Malcolm told him it was time to close up shop for the day.

"Already?" asked Mikey, genuinely surprised that it was closing time. "But I just got here."

"You've been working non-stop since you walked in the front door. Believe me, you've done enough for your first day, and I promised your mom I'd walk you home this evening."

While locking up, Malcolm asked "Are you hungry?"

"I suppose so." said Mikey, looking down and away from Mr. Abernathy.

"How about we grab a couple of subs from Maggie's deli on the way to your house. You can surprise your mom with dinner tonight," said Malcolm.

"That would be nice," Mikey replied. "It's been kind of hard on Mom since Dad left, so she doesn't cook as often as she did before she went overseas."

Malcolm bought three subs along with some potato salad and coleslaw before walking Mikey the rest of the way home. At the door, he took one sandwich out of the bag and left the rest for Mikey and his mother.

"Tell your mother I said hello, and that you did a great job today," said Malcolm, adding "I'll see you tomorrow at 3:00 p.m. sharp, okay?"

"Yes Sir," said Mikey. "Thank you for everything, Mr. Abernathy."

It didn't take long for Mikey to develop a routine, systematically cleaning the shop from top to bottom. After the first week, you'd have been hard-pressed to find a single speck of dust in the entire shop, and the shelves were more organized than they had ever been. That evening at Mikey's front door, along with an extra-large pizza and some cinnamon bites, Malcolm gave Mikey an envelope containing four crisp, new twenty-dollar bills.

Before going inside, Mikey asked "Can I come to work for you on Saturdays, Mr. Abernathy?"

"Are you sure you don't need a day off, young man?" asked Malcolm. "You've been putting in a lot of work for me."

"I like coming to work for you, Mr. Abernathy," said Mikey. "I've learned a lot of things there, and the people who come to your shop are really nice to me. Besides, I never do anything on Saturday anyway."

"Then, I guess I'll see you tomorrow," said Malcolm. "Tell your mom, I said hello," he added before turning to head back. He'd only taken a couple of steps before he heard the door open again and turned to find Mrs. Anderson standing in the doorway.

"Mr. Abernathy..." she said. "I just want to thank you for everything."

"Oh, you have nothing to thank me for. That Mikey is a godsend," said Malcolm. "I've never seen a young man work so hard, and I'm happy to have him around."

"He talks about you all the time," said Heidi. "He's like a different person since meeting you, and I'm grateful to you for taking him in and making him feel welcome."

"He *is* welcome, Mrs. Anderson; just as you are, anytime you'd like to come by," said Malcolm.

"Thank you." she said. "I may even take you up on that offer soon."

"Please do," said Malcolm, before tipping his hat and saying, "Good evening, Mrs. Anderson."

As he headed back, he had to smile to himself. Heidi had actually taken a small step beyond the threshold of her doorway today. Perhaps, she was also one step closer to paying Mikey a visit at the shop.

Coco's puppysitter didn't work on weekends, so Malcolm would bring the little Pomeranian to work with him. She was a bit withdrawn when it came to other people, so she usually stayed hidden away in his office for most of the day.

It had been a slow afternoon, so Coco was sitting on the corner of Malcolm's workbench when Mikey walked in. Entering right behind him, was Heidi.

Quickly standing and walking over to them, Malcolm warmly shook her hand before making a grand entrance gesture with his open arms, saying "Welcome to I FIX BROKEN THINGS. What can I fix for *you* today?"

"That's exactly what Mikey said you would say," Heidi stated with a smile, as Mikey donned his apron and disappeared into the shelves with his broom in hand. "I thought I would come by for a short visit. I hope I'm not intruding, and I'll understand if it's not a good time for you."

"Nonsense!" exclaimed Malcolm with a smile, stepping aside to usher her into the shop. In that very instant, something amazing happened.

Coco, who had been lying beside Malcolm all morning long and ignoring everyone, suddenly sat up, tilting her head to the side when she noticed Heidi. The two of them seemed completely engrossed in one another as Heidi slowly approached Coco who was still sitting motionless at the workbench.

Malcolm watched, incredulously as Heidi drew nearer and Coco remained seated there in total silence. His little Pomeranian had always been a yapper, intolerant of everyone and everything except for Malcolm. The mere fact that she wasn't barking as if the apocalypse was upon her was amazing enough to Malcolm; however, when Heidi reached the workbench and slowly extended her hand, Coco licked it! A few seconds later, she jumped right into Heidi's arms!

Malcolm didn't utter a single word as he watched in sheer disbelief, the scene unfolding right before his very eyes. Turning to face Malcolm, Heidi asked "What is her name?"

"Coco... Her name is Coco," said Malcolm slowly, as if he were witnessing the birth of a new sun.

"May I hold onto her while I look around?" asked Heidi.

Malcolm nodded wordlessly as the two of them disappeared down one of the aisles together. After a moment he said "Well, I'll be damned. Now I've seen everything."

Chapter Seven

The year's first snowfall came in November, and along with it, the holiday season. Malcolm was going to need help in order to manage the rush, realizing how sometimes, the best gifts are those things we love but can no longer use.

Restoring something the owner already loves, is much different than trying to guess what they might need. Such things are familiar and proven, and those receiving them already know how they work and what they're used for.

The shop's glowing reputation combined with the increased intake volume of the holiday season, soon overwhelmed Malcolm. While he was incredibly fast at making the repairs, he couldn't keep up with the pace of clients coming through the door. If his reputation were going to survive the next three months, he would need to hire someone.

Just as that realization came to him, Mikey and his mother walked through the door. Since their first encounter, Heidi and Coco had developed an interesting bond. Every Saturday morning, Malcolm would bring Coco to work with him, and by 3:00 p.m. she was sitting next to the front door waiting for Heidi to arrive.

For Heidi, Malcolm's shop was something of a refuge. She could disappear between the shelves for hours, and with Coco in her arms, she was surprisingly at ease. Shortly before closing time, the two of them would reappear and Malcolm would walk Mikey and Heidi back home, where she would reluctantly hand Coco back over to Malcolm.

That morning, before they could disappear into the catacombs, Malcolm said "Heidi, would you consider working for me? I could really use the help, and I'd be happy to pay you whatever you need to make it worth your while."

With her back still to him, she buried her face in Coco's soft fur. It was a full minute before she turned to face Malcolm, softly asking "What would you need me to do?"

"You'd only need to do intake," said Malcolm. "Just write down the date and time along with the client's contact information on a tag and attach it to whatever they need fixed. Then, you can put it on the shelf over near my workbench and I'll take care of the rest."

"That's all?" asked Heidi.

"That's all," said Malcolm. "If you'd like to do more as you get comfortable working here, you can; but I'll leave that totally up to you."

"Okay," said Heidi, before asking "When would you like me to start?"

"How does Monday sound?" asked Malcolm.

Smiling, Heidi said "Okay," before disappearing between the shelves with Coco again.

Captain Heidi Anderson had been an Air Force Logistics Readiness Officer. Although her husband was always supportive of her career, as a civilian, he was somewhat naive when it came to the inherent risks of serving in the armed forces.

Afghanistan had been her first overseas tour, and while it was difficult leaving her son and husband behind, she proudly answered the call to serve her country upon receiving her deployment orders. As a flight commander, she was responsible for the supply lines supporting forward-deployed US and allied troops.

Although her unit was located well inside the supposed green zone, her career ended abruptly when a mortar round struck the warehouse where she was conducting an inventory. Fortunately, she'd been facing away from the blast when it occurred. *Unfortunately*, it sent shrapnel ripping into her body from tailbone to shoulders, leaving permanent scars both physically and emotionally.

It took a month for her to emerge from the coma, and even longer before she could walk again. By the time she was released from Landstuhl Army Medical Center, her marriage was hanging by a thread, and when her husband realized the scars on her back would never fade, that thread broke.

She left the Air Force on a medical retirement, and returned to Idaho with Mikey, hoping to find serenity in the simplistic lifestyle of Mountain Home. Instead, she became a borderline recluse—rarely, if ever, leaving the house for more than a few minutes each month.

Unbeknownst to Malcolm, her excursions into the aisles of his establishment had not been for nothing. For weeks, she'd been cataloging the contents and locations of every item on his shelves, and by the time he got around to offering her a job, the database she'd been working on, was complete.

She was waiting at the side door of the shop when Malcolm arrived on Monday morning. To his surprise, she was exceptionally well prepared after having spent the weekend creating an intake spreadsheet that would streamline and standardize the entire process.

In addition to the spreadsheet, she uploaded inventory and accounting programs to his computer system, making it easier to match the items repaired, to the people who'd brought them in. Needless to say, within five minutes of her arrival, Malcolm was already seriously impressed.

As the day progressed, Malcolm kept an eye on her, making sure that she wasn't getting overwhelmed, but by the time Mikey showed up at 3:00 p.m., Heidi was totally in her element. Not only was Malcolm able to get more repairs done, he didn't have to stop working to notify customers that their items were ready. By the end of her first workday, Malcolm had more than doubled his productivity, and thanks to Mikey, the shop was as clean as a whistle.

"The two of you are an amazing team," said Malcolm while walking them home. As Mikey ran ahead of them, Malcolm added, "I am very fortunate to have both of you helping me."

"I guess we're all equally fortunate," said Heidi. "Mikey likes you very much, and he really looks up to you."

"He's a good kid," said Malcolm with a smile. "and you've done a great job raising him."

"Not really," said Heidi. "There are so many things I wish I could have done better, but Mikey hung in there with me anyway." Stopping at their front door, she turned to face Malcolm, saying "You're a good man, Mr. Abernathy. Thank you for hanging in there with *both* of us."

With a smile and tip of his hat, Malcolm said "Goodnight, Mrs. Anderson. I'll see you in the morning."

"Goodnight, Mr. Abernathy," Heidi replied, closing the door between them. Leaning back against it, she exhaled while sliding down to sit on the floor.

"We can do this, Heidi," she whispered to herself. "We can do this."

The human brain is one of the most complex things on Earth. It is both fragile and resilient. It can both de-generate and re-generate. While one activity can send it careening into darkness, another can bring it swiftly back to life. In people suffering from PTSD, the line separating those extremes is often razor thin.

For years, Heidi had spent hours each day, meticulously tracking everything around her. Malcolm's shop was significantly smaller than a military warehouse, but its contents were much more diverse, and for Heidi, the sweet spot between overwhelming and revitalizing, was now called I FIX BROKEN THINGS.

Chapter Eight

With his three-person crew in place, Malcolm's business was booming! He'd always been a top-notch repairman, but with the extra time he gained from having Heidi and Mikey managing the business flow and keeping things neat and orderly, he was able to complete twice as many repairs in the same amount of time.

"Tomorrow is Thanksgiving Day," said Heidi.

Glancing up from his workbench, Malcolm noticed she and Mikey were there looking at him. "Indeed, it is," he said. "and you two have given me a lot to be thankful for. How about we close up early today, and meet back here on Friday?"

"Well, Mikey and I were wondering what you and Coco have planned for tomorrow, and if you'd like to join us for dinner?" said Heidi.

"We haven't really made any plans," said Malcolm. "We've been so busy, I haven't had time to think about it; but yes, we'd be happy to join you."

"I was hoping you'd say that," said Heidi with a smile. "Otherwise, we'd have concocted a plan to kidnap both of you." Thinking it over, she added "Actually, we'd only need to kidnap you. I'm fairly sure Coco would be a willing accomplice."

"No doubt about it," said Malcolm. "She's a sucker for table food."

"Then, Mikey and I will expect you around 1:00 p.m. so we can eat, and then you boys can watch the game afterwards," said Heidi.

"Food **and** football?" said Malcolm. "My list of things to be thankful for, just got longer."

Turning off the light over his workbench, Malcolm stood up, saying "Well, let's lock up and get a head start on tomorrow."

As always, Malcolm walked them home and bid them farewell at the door. Before disappearing inside, Heidi said "We'll see you tomorrow, Mr. Abernathy. Bring your appetite with you because I'll be cooking enough to feed a small army."

"Yes Ma'am," he answered, "But please, call me Malcolm. I don't plan on being an employer on Thanksgiving Day; only a friend."

"Okay, Malcolm," she said. "See you tomorrow."

As she closed the door, Malcolm tipped his hat and smiled before walking back to his car in the parking lot behind his shop. On his way home, he stopped at a flower shop to purchase a bouquet for Heidi.

When the florist asked, "What type of bouquet are you looking for, Mr. Abernathy?"

Malcolm responded, "Oh, something nice that shows I appreciate her."

"Are you looking for an arrangement that's strictly platonic, or perhaps something more?"

For the first time in as far back as he could remember, Malcolm was at a loss for words. Of course, what he felt for Heidi was more than strictly platonic. In the space of a few months, she and Mikey had completely changed his life. He could remember the smell of her shampoo and clearly recall the sound of her laughter. She and Mikey were the two people he saw nearly every day, and on Sunday evening, he was already looking forward to Monday morning, when he'd see them again.

Coco adored Heidi, as if signaling to Malcolm, "This is the one, Papa. This is the one that we want," and while he never made it obvious, he'd catch himself watching her as she walked around the shop welcoming customers and logging in their items.

It was then he realized, nothing about his feelings for either of them was strictly platonic. He truly adored Heidi, and Mikey was like a son to him. The only question which remained unanswered, was "What the hell kind of bouquet says that!?"

As the smiling florist patiently waited for him to define the nature of their relationship, Malcolm said "She is like the smell of approaching rain on a warm summer day. Her voice is the lullaby sung to a child while safe inside his mother's embrace. When she laughs, it's sincere and undiluted and when she's worried or afraid, it feels natural that I would protect her with my very life. She is strong yet fragile, broken but far from incomplete, and while life has caused her to forget how beautiful she is, I see it every time my eyes are fortunate enough to light upon her.

"So, definitely *not* strictly platonic," said the Florist. "I'll tell you what. Let me put something together for you first thing in the morning after the fresh flowers are delivered, and you can pick them up before we close at noon."

"That sounds good," said Malcolm. "I'll trust your judgement, and I'm sure the bouquet you create will be perfect."

"You can be sure of that, Mr. Abernathy," said the florist with a smile. "You fixed my mom's grandfather clock when everyone else told her it wasn't worth the effort. That clock meant the world to her, and when she discovered it was working again, she was happier than I'd ever seen her before. I promise you that Mrs. Anderson will understand exactly how you feel the moment she sees her flowers."

"Thank you very much," said Malcolm. "I will see you before noon tomorrow."

During the remainder of his short drive home, his thoughts had no central theme, but Heidi and Mikey were the common thread that ran through all of them. For the very first Thanksgiving in his life, Malcolm had a family with which to spend it.

On Thanksgiving Day, he arrived at Heidi's and Mikey's front door at 12:45 p.m. The look in Heidi's eyes when she saw the colossal flower arrangement was one of sheer amazement. In keeping with her word, the florist had outdone herself and vastly exceeded any expectations Malcolm could possibly have ever imagined.

The arrangement was created inside a handwoven cornucopia and contained one dozen red roses, one dozen golden roses, six orange and yellow giant mums, and a dozen large tiger lilies. They were arranged atop a bed of golden-yellow wheat helms, and dried corn husks. Yellow baby's breath was interspersed among the larger flowers, along with ten miniature cat tails. It was the most amazing flower arrangement Malcolm had ever seen, and it was obvious, Heidi loved it.

As she removed the cellophane wrapping and placed it on the dining room table, Malcolm took a moment to look around the dining- and living-room areas with Mikey. For someone who many might call reclusive, Heidi kept her home very neat and beautifully organized. In fact, their modest single-story house reminded him of a model home used to showcase the floorplans of a new housing development. Even though everything was in its proper place, the home felt warm and welcoming.

Returning to Heidi in the dining-room, Malcolm discovered how the bouquet had expanded once the cellophane wrapper was removed. What he had overlooked was the envelope tucked away inside the arrangement. He had no idea it was there until Heidi pulled it out and opened it. Since Malcolm hadn't chosen a card, he was a bit nervous when she opened it and softly began to read aloud. Halfway through it, she turned her back to him. For a moment he was terrified, because he could tell she was crying even though she was facing away from him.

Inside the card, the florist had written:

> *"You are like the smell of approaching rain on a warm summer day. Your voice is the*

lullaby sung to a child held safe inside his mother's embrace. Your laughter is sincere and undiluted, and when you are worried or afraid, it feels natural that I would protect you with my very life. You are strong yet fragile, broken but far from incomplete, and while life has caused you to forget how beautiful you are, I see it every time my eyes are fortunate enough to light upon you."

Malcolm was flabbergasted! While he immediately recognized the words, he spoken to the florist, he had no idea she'd actually remembered them and written them down, nearly verbatim.

After a moment, she wiped her eyes and turned to face him, asking "Malcolm, do you really mean all of these things?"

"Yes," replied Malcolm. "I do."

"It's the most beautiful thing anyone's ever said to me. I... I don't know what to say," Heidi said, trying her best not to cry in front of him.

"Happy Thanksgiving, Heidi," said Malcolm, opening his arms and hugging her as she laid her head against his chest. "You and Mikey are the closest thing to a family that I've got, and I honestly love both of you very much."

"Happy Thanksgiving, Malcolm," replied Heidi. "Thank you for rescuing us." After a brief pause, she said "Now, let's eat before I totally fall to pieces."

Needless to say, dinner was delicious. From the tender, juicy roasted turkey, and stuffing, to the pasta salad, green bean casserole and potatoes au gratin, the meal was nothing short of amazing. The sweet-potato pie served with vanilla ice-cream for dessert, added the crowning touch to a perfect meal.

Although Malcolm offered to help put everything away and clean up the kitchen, Heidi insisted he join Mikey in the living room to enjoy the Football game. Despite their best efforts, by the time Heidi finished cleaning up and came into the living room with Coco close behind her, both Malcolm and Mikey were asleep at opposite ends of the couch.

Smiling, she sat between the two of them, pulling up her feet and leaning her head against Malcolm, who put his arm around her. Coco claimed her spot behind Heidi's knees, and within minutes all of them were asleep.

Malcolm awoke around 10:00 p.m. with Heidi and Coco still asleep next to him on the couch. Mikey had gone to bed about an hour earlier, and as much as he loved being there with them, he thought it best that he and Coco head home before it got too late. He woke Heidi with a kiss on her forehead, saying that he and Coco needed to get going.

Reluctantly, Heidi walked with them to the door. Before opening it, she handed him a bag of leftovers packed inside sealed plastic containers saying, "Thank you for a beautiful Thanksgiving, Malcolm."

"Thank you for the invitation," he replied. "You and Mikey mean the world to us," he added, picking up

Coco and including her in the declaration. "Get some rest. There's no need opening the shop before noon tomorrow, so we're going to sleep in too."

Before he could say another word, she pulled his face to hers and kissed him. After several seconds, their lips slowly parted and she said, "That was for the beautiful flowers. You are such an amazing man, Malcolm."

"And you, my dear, are nothing short of wonderful," he replied, opening the door, and stepping outside with Coco under his arm. "Goodnight, Heidi."

"Goodnight," she said, watching until the two of them disappeared around the corner and into the night.

Chapter Nine

Despite his stated intention of sleeping in, on Friday morning, Malcolm was awake at 6:00 a.m., just as he was every other morning. He dressed in his thermal running gear and headed out the back door of his spacious, secluded home, into the snowy landscape surrounding it.

Malcolm had always wanted to live in a log cabin. Growing up in a place like Youngstown, Ohio, that dream was a certain impossibility, and he joined the Navy on his eighteenth birthday, just to get away from there.

As a Navy SEAL, very few of his assignments ever put him near locations where a log cabin would have been practical. However, even while slipping in and out of the Red Sea during covert operations in the Middle East, that dream of a snow-covered cabin nestled inside a thick stand of tall pine trees, was a happy place to which his thoughts always returned.

After more than sixteen years conducting active operations, Malcolm had been shot, stabbed, and nearly blown up on more than one occasion. His body was a living testament to violence, bearing the scars of conflicts from around the world. During his final covert mission near Damascus, he was captured by radical militants who intended to execute him in a live-streaming propaganda video. He escaped after killing everyone in the room with the same knife they intended to use in beheading him, then announced his location coordinates using the live video stream they, *themselves,* had established. Twenty minutes later, he was aboard a Naval helicopter with his fellow SEALS, as F-18 Hornets laid waste to the compound where his captors had been holding him.

In order to preserve mission integrity, heroes involved in covert operations abroad are not officially recognized. Accordingly, Senior Chief Malcom Abernathy received his Congressional Medal of Honor from the President during a private ceremony inside the Oval Office at the White House.

Malcolm continued serving as a training instructor for another five years before retiring, and a few months later he'd purchased his log cabin, and was on the way to Idaho. Much like Heidi, Malcolm wanted to disappear for a little while and simply find himself again. He'd been living outside Mountain Home for over a year when he noticed the vacancy sign in the window of the empty shop.

Acting on a whim, he signed the lease not even knowing what he would do with the space. It took another six months before he decided to open a repair shop for unusual items, and he'd actually come up with the name for it while waiting in line at City Hall for his business license.

Malcolm started his day the same way each morning, running a seven-mile course through the woods around his cabin, come rain or shine. Afterwards, he ate a hearty breakfast with Coco, reviewed the security feeds covering the shop, and scoured local ads and internet auction sites for unusual items.

While in the Navy, he'd maintained his affinity for collecting and fixing things, and had items stashed away in multiple storage facilities around the country. Upon signing the lease for his shop, he had everything moved there which explained the strange variety of odds and ends on the shelves.

That particular Friday morning, he sat at the bar in his kitchen thinking about Heidi and Mikey as he sipped his coffee. Having made a career, living in the center of absolute violence, Malcolm had never been married. Somehow, he felt it wasn't right asking someone to commit to him, realizing they would worry constantly, never knowing if he'd be coming home again after any given mission. Now, for the first time in his life, he felt as if he truly mattered to someone, and they most definitely mattered to him!

After making a few phone calls, he took his time getting to work on Friday, arriving shortly after 10:30 a.m. to turn on the lights and get a fresh pot of coffee brewing. The silver sedan parked across the street wouldn't have been cause for alarm to most people, but Malcolm had noticed it earlier, while reviewing the shop's security feeds during breakfast. His intuition regarding such things had served him well over the years, and he wasn't going to start ignoring it now.

The surveillance cameras covering the front of the shop were able to zoom in closely on the two men inside the vehicle, and Malcolm took several crystal-clear images of both the driver and the passenger.

Once the coffee was ready, he filled two Styrofoam cups and covered them with plastic lids. Thinking it over, he grabbed a few packets of sweetener and a couple of miniature creamer tubs before walking out the front door, across the street and right up to the driver's side of the car. After setting the coffee and accompaniments on top of the car, he tapped on the window.

Obviously irritated, the driver lowered the window, staring at Malcolm with an angry scowl across his lips. Before he could say anything, Malcolm said, "You guys look like you could use some coffee."

Oddly enough, no matter where you find yourself in the world, people's natural reaction when offered a cup of coffee, is to take it. Not surprisingly, both men accepted the cups as Malcolm reached in through the window.

"I've been watching you from my store for a few minutes now, and it seems like whoever you're waiting for isn't coming—unless, of course, you're waiting for me," Malcolm said with a smile.

Using a slow, measured tone, the driver said, "You're a strange man, Mr. Abernathy. Most people wouldn't be so relaxed after costing my boss a half-million dollars."

"You must be mistaking me with a different Mr. Abernathy, or possibly with the guy from the sportsbook down the street," Malcolm answered with a sarcastic smile.

"Nope," said the driver, holding up a photo of Malcolm taken through his shop window. "I'm fairly sure this is you. What do you think, Lenny?"

"Looks like this Jerk, right here, to me," answered Lenny.

"It does bear a striking resemblance to me," said Malcolm, "but I don't owe anyone a nickel, so unless your boss's name is Uncle Sam, and he's sending IRS agents out for collection calls now, you dogs are barking up the wrong tree."

"Nathan said you were a cocky SOB, but he didn't mention that you were also a comedian," said the driver. "Hey, Lenny, did he mention to you that this guy's a comedian?"

"Nope. Not to me," answered Lenny.

Turning back to Malcolm, the driver said "Listen, Mr. Abernathy, we know it was you, who set up Nathan to get busted with the boss's money and merchandise in his truck. Now, as far as I'm concerned, your beef with Nathan, was between you and him; but the money didn't belong to Nathan, and now the boss wants it back. Do you see where I'm going with this, Mr. Abernathy?"

"To be perfectly honest, no, I don't," said Malcolm. "According to the news reports, Nathan was stopped for speeding down the middle of Main Street and then showing his ass when the cop pulled him over, instead of just accepting the ticket. Sounds to me like your boss's problem starts and ends with Nathan. Perhaps you should be having this conversation with him."

"Unfortunately, Nathan didn't hold up very well during our conversation with him, did he, Lenny?" said the driver.

"Nope," said Lenny. "He didn't hold up very well at all, but maybe Mr. Comedy Club here could fix that broken neck you gave him. What do you think?"

"Now, that's a show I'd pay to see!" said the driver, laughing hysterically before his face turned as cold as ice. Looking at Malcolm again, he said "Mr. Abernathy, thanks for the coffee. Lenny and I will each chip in a buck towards the balance you owe, but we will be back on Monday to settle up. You got that?"

"I don't know. Did you get that, Sherriff?" said Malcolm.

Suddenly, there were Sherriff's cruisers pouring into the street from both directions, surrounding the silver sedan as Malcolm backed away with both hands in the air.

"Enjoy the coffee, boys," said Malcolm, waving at the two men as police officers closed in on them with weapons drawn. From inside the store, he watched through the window as they were placed under arrest and loaded into the backseats of separate cruisers. Ten minutes later, every sign that they had even been there, was gone.

After the commotion died down, Malcolm spoke briefly with Sherriff Baker to make sure the audio and video recordings were clean. On the bottom of the paper coffee cups, he'd attached small radio transmitters. They looked similar to the little round bandages used to cover shaving nicks and had a range of a quarter mile. They're effective because most people would never think of tipping over a cup of hot coffee to check the bottom of it; especially sitting inside a car.

After the call, he was ready to put the entire episode behind him, and while seated at his desk, he noticed Heidi approaching on the feed covering the side entrance. Timing it perfectly, He opened the door just as she reached for the doorknob, catching her off-guard and pulling her inside.

A moment later, they were kissing passionately and holding onto one another as if their lives depended upon it. It was the first time they'd been alone since that Thanksgiving Day kiss, and it took every ounce of their resolve to allow the moment to end with just a kiss.

Peeling themselves apart, Heidi spoke first, saying "You know; I think I need to cook dinner for you more often."

"I second that motion," said Malcolm with a smile. "but how about letting me cook for you next time?"

"I like the sound of that," said Heidi before asking, "Are there any more surprises hidden up your sleeve?"

"Dozens," said Malcolm. "How about you and Mikey pack a few things, and come spend the weekend with me and Coco? We'll close up shop and spend some time getting to know each other *much* better."

"I'd like that," said Heidi "but what if we don't want to leave anymore."

"Then, my plan will have worked out perfectly," said Malcolm.

Their first customer was waiting by the front door when Malcolm opened the shop at high noon, and the steady intake of items for repair kept both of them busy. Nevertheless, the smiles and stolen glances they shared with one another throughout the day were obviously those of two people, already deeply in love.

As always, Malcolm walked Heidi and Mikey home that evening. Even though they didn't notice it, He was quietly observing everything around them. After nearly a year at his shop, he knew every vehicle, entrepreneur, pedestrian, and regular visitor to the diner across the street. His experienced eye detected everything that seemed out of place and assessed its potential as a threat.

While there were no apparent anomalies, Malcolm was well-aware of how thugs and their bosses operated. Until he was sure they wouldn't try to retaliate, he'd keep an eye on everything, just to be on the safe side.

Although Malcolm's public-facing identity was that of someone a bit out of step with reality, the façade was a carefully constructed one. He wanted people to connect his appearance with the services he offered, without it being cause for alarm. People tend to notice extravagant individuals at first, but then quickly write them off as nuts, and forget all about them.

For Malcolm, being seen as the strange guy from the repair shop made it easy for him to hide in plain sight—something impossible for a Medal of Honor recipient who'd freed himself and four other servicemembers, while killing his way out of a terrorist training compound on the Arabian Peninsula. Following that mission, he'd been reassigned as a training instructor because of the Caliphate's bounty on his head.

Malcolm's cover was harmless, but the man behind it was nothing to be trifled with. Prior to removing the boards covering the storefront, Malcolm had installed ballistic glass windows, and replaced the crumbling interior sheetrock with one-inch-thick steel plating. In addition, he'd installed a carbon dioxide fire suppression system that would instantly extinguish any ignition source within the structure. His office, equipped with closed-circuit monitors and an independent wireless communication system, was literally a vault inside a fortress, and once it was locked down, there was no way into, or out of it.

The lower level of Malcom's home had received similar upgrades after he purchased it, and nothing short of an Air Force bunker-buster would even put a dent in it. One benefit of a log cabin is that logs are natural barriers capable of stopping projectiles fired from most small arms weaponry—something early pioneers found most useful in defending against hostile raids and attacks. It wasn't the reason Malcolm loved log cabins, but it was definitely something he loved about them.

After the clear message conveyed by the two goons outside Malcolm's shop, he wanted to be sure Heidi and Mikey were safe, without unnecessarily frightening them. From the security of his house, he could monitor the shop remotely while keeping the two people he held most dear, out of harm's way. After a few days, he would have a better idea as to whether or not additional measures would be necessary.

The drive up to Malcolm's house reminded Heidi of a trip to the North Pole, and as they approached the gate to his property, it opened to reveal the completion of that image. Mikey's eyes widened at the site of the sprawling house nestled inside the grove of snow-covered pine trees.

As they passed by the front of the house and continued down a gravel driveway to the left of the building, the size of Malcolm's home came more clearly into view. What appeared to be a large one-story house from the front, had two additional floors which were only visible from the rear, and the entire back wall of the house was made of glass.

"Wow!" said Mikey, exiting the truck. "This is the coolest house ever!"

"Well, I'm glad you like it," said Malcolm with a smile as he opened the door for Heidi.

"You are just full of surprises, Mr. Abernathy!" exclaimed Heidi, smiling as she walked around the back of the truck to take in the entire view of the magnificent house. Shaking her head, she joked, "Don't tell me. Let me guess. Your real name is Santa Claus, isn't it?"

"Uh Oh," said Malcolm. "I guess my cover's blown," After taking a few minutes for them to admire the house, he said "Come on in. Let me give you the grand tour."

They followed Malcolm into the house through the garage, totally amazed at both the size and layout of each floor as they progressed upward. The kitchen, dining area, and living room were all located on the top floor, which, all by itself, would have been the equivalent of a mansion for most people.

While Heidi and Mikey made themselves comfortable, Malcolm brought in their overnight bags and the groceries he'd purchased earlier that day. Not surprisingly to Heidi, Malcolm was as skilled in the kitchen as he was at his workbench in the shop. Within an hour, he'd prepared a delicious meal for them, that they enjoyed while looking out across the snowy landscape behind this dream of a house.

After dinner, Malcolm showed each of them to their bedrooms on the second level, where Mikey became immediately engrossed in the gaming console and sixty-five inch flat-screen monitor, asking "Mom, can I please stay here for a while and play video games? This is so awesome!"

"As long as Malcolm doesn't mind," she said.

"Don't mind me," said Malcolm. "Knock yourself out; it's your room."

By the time they slipped out of the room and closed the door behind them, Mikey was already immersed in his video game.

In the Den on the lower level, Malcolm and Heidi settled in on the sofa across from the fireplace. She leaned her head against him, and he wrapped his arm around her shoulder.

They spoke for hours, revealing more of themselves to each other than they'd ever shared with anyone. Heidi explained how her marriage had ended only days after her being released from the hospital, and how she and Mikey had somehow managed to struggle through it together. Malcolm revealed the darkest corners of his life to Heidi and explained how he hoped living in a quiet place like Mountain Home would allow him to leave the ghosts of his past, behind him.

Turning to face her, Malcolm said "I've spent over half of my life, doubting that I would ever find you. Now, here you are more beautiful than I ever imagined, right here in my arms."

"No, Malcolm," said Heidi. "I'm not beautiful. As much as I'd like to be, even if only for you, I'm not."

"Heidi, you just don't see..." started Malcolm before she softly cut him off.

"Malcolm, please," said Heidi. "I spent all of last night, wishing I could awaken this morning as that beautiful woman you described in your card, but I didn't, and I know I never will."

Standing up, she turned and walked toward the fireplace. With her back to him, she unbuttoned her shirt and let it slide slowly from her shoulders to the floor. Covering her face with her hands, she stood there, silently weeping.

From her shoulders down to her lower back, she was covered with scars and burn marks left by shrapnel from the grenade blast that had nearly killed her in Afghanistan. Despite her feelings for Malcolm, she would rather face his rejection now, before totally losing her heart to him.

As she stood there in silence, she was surprised by the gentle touch of his fingertips as they lightly traced the tapestry of scars adorning her back. His strong hands gently encircled her waist, and she felt his lips on her shoulders before he slowly kissed his way down to her lower back.

When he rose to his feet again, she turned to face him. He'd removed his shirt, revealing a chiseled torso covered with old scar tissue. Leaning forward, she kissed the long slash across his chest as she reached around him, feeling the uneven pattern of scars and puncture wounds also covering his back.

There were tears streaming down her face when she looked up into his eyes, saying "Malcolm, my love. You are beautiful too."

There in the den, illuminated by the glow of the fireplace, they finally unleashed the passion that had been building between them for so long. By the time they fell asleep in each other's arms, the roaring fire had been reduced to glowing embers, and freshly fallen snow quietly blanketed the grounds outside, just beyond the window.

Chapter Ten

The next morning Malcolm felt as if he could've run all the way to Boise. Heidi was awake by the time he made it back to the house, and from the path where he emerged from the woods, he could see her upstairs in the kitchen through the window. She was wearing the shirt he'd taken off in the den the night before and he smiled at the sight of her walking across the heated floors on her bare feet.

As he ran up the driveway around to the front of the house, he couldn't help but feel Heidi and Mikey belonged there. That big empty house was made for a family larger than only Coco and him, and it finally felt like home.

Heidi met him at the front door, saying "I can honestly say, I've never had a man literally run out of the house after making love to me."

Taking Heidi in his arms, Malcolm kissed her before saying, "But, I will always come running right back to you."

"Great come-back, Mr. Abernathy," said Heidi, smiling at him over her shoulder as she turned and tiptoed back into the kitchen. "I made breakfast."

"I know. I saw you in the kitchen when I came up from the back of the house," he replied. "It had my mouth watering."

"You could smell breakfast cooking all the way out there?" she asked.

"Who said anything about breakfast?" he answered with a smile.

Just then, Mikey came up the stairs into the kitchen. "Good morning, Mom. Good morning, Malcolm," he said. "It really smells good in here!"

"Good morning, Mikey," said Malcolm. "Did you reach Gunship level twenty yet?"

"Twenty-six," said Mikey with a grin. "I didn't want to stop before I caught up to you."

"Impressive!" said Malcolm with a nod of acknowledgement.

"Oh, Lord," said Heidi. "Now I have two gamers to deal with."

"Like you said, Mom. It's better than having me out there, running the crazy streets of Mountain Home."

"Who knows when you might run into a warlock or something?" added Malcolm with a grin.

"I have no idea what either of you are talking about," said Heidi with a sheepish grin. "Look! Pancakes!" she added, quickly changing the subject.

Malcolm's sense of contentment was obvious as he sat enjoying breakfast with Heidi and Mikey. Afterwards, he took them hiking through the woods surrounding his property, pointing out different species of birds, vegetation and wildlife that were indigenous to the area.

On the way back to the house, Mikey pointed to the branches of one of the trees, asking "What is that for?"

Looking up, Malcolm said "This tree is one of the markers for my property line. Since cameras are a lot less intrusive than fences, I use them at different points along the perimeter so I can monitor everything without interfering in nature's balance."

"Wow! That is so cool!" exclaimed Mikey. "You mean, you can see everything around here from your house?"

"Yep," said Malcolm. "As a matter of fact, you can watch every camera around the property from the gaming monitor in your room, or any other television in the house. Just go to input three."

"Really?" said Mikey. "That is so cool! Can you show me when we get inside?"

"Of course," said Malcolm. "It's always good to know what's going on around you. Besides, it's a hundred times better than the Nature Channel."

As Mikey ran ahead of them back to the house, Heidi said "You did mention you had dozens of surprises up your sleeve," said Heidi. "Once again, I'm impressed."

"Sometimes, bad experiences can make you a bit over-cautious," said Malcolm. "I guess, in that sense, we're a lot alike."

"We are," said Heidi. "but I always feel safe with you. It's like I can relax, knowing you're there watching over us."

Taking both of her hands in his, Malcolm said "I love you, Heidi. I love both of you, and I will never let anyone or anything harm either of you. I promise."

"I know," said Heidi. "For the first time in my life, I really *know* that."

As they walked into the house, Mikey called out "Hey, Malcolm. Come check this out!" Following him into his room upstairs, Malcolm and Heidi saw that he had the camera feed from the shop displayed on his monitor screen. "It looks like that guy is trying to get into the shop!"

"It does, doesn't it?" said Malcolm. "You wanna see what happens next?"

"Sure," said Mikey, excitedly.

"Do you see that red circle at the bottom right-hand corner of the screen?" asked Malcolm.

"Yeah," said Mikey. "should I click on it?"

"Yep," said Malcolm. "Then, watch the timer that appears just above it."

Mikey clicked on the button, and the three of them watched the timer on the screen. It only took thirty-eight seconds for the security firm to drive by the building and illuminate him with a spotlight. Upon noticing he was being watched, he walked off down the sidewalk as if he were just out for a stroll. The security vehicle followed him until he was well clear of the building, before killing the spotlight and driving away.

"That was fast!" said Heidi. "Do they always arrive so quickly?"

"Well, they guarantee a response in under sixty seconds, but most of the time, they arrive in under forty-five seconds," said Malcolm.

"What if the guy had made it inside?" asked Mikey.

"That wouldn't be possible," said Malcolm. "Without a special key, they couldn't open the door, and if the security system isn't deactivated within fifteen seconds of entering the building, the door shuts behind them and the authorities are notified. Even if the Sherriff doesn't respond as quickly, the security firm will still arrive within sixty seconds."

"That's like something out of a secret agent movie," said Mikey. "Did you put in all of that stuff yourself?"

"As a matter of fact, I did," said Malcolm. "I guess you could say, it's sort of a hobby of mine."

Malcolm showed Heidi and Mikey around, explaining the ins and outs of the house, and how they should react in the event of an emergency. He also showed them how to activate the auxiliary power in the event of a blackout and entered their biometrics into the security system.

"What if someone just breaks a window?" asked Mikey. "Except for the garage door, the whole back of the house is made of glass."

"Come on," said Malcolm. "I'll show you something."

Exiting the house through the garage, Malcolm grabbed his baseball bat and batting helmet, asking "Do you like baseball, Mikey?"

"Sure." said Mikey, before asking "Why?"

"Well, let me show you how I work on my swing." answered Malcolm with a smile.

Walking over to the area just outside the den, he pulled the tarp off of a baseball pitching machine with a dozen or so balls in the hopper. After plugging it into an extension cord running from the garage, he walked about sixty feet out into the backyard and swept away some of the snow, revealing a regulation size home plate on the ground facing the house. Directly behind it stretched between two trees, was a mesh net about ten feet high. With Mikey standing safely behind the net, he activated the pitching machine.

"The countdown clock gives you thirty seconds to get in place, and then it'll shoot a ball this way about every seven seconds."

Sure enough, the first ball flew towards the plate and Malcolm's swing connected, sending it harmlessly into the glass about halfway up the wall. From inside the house, you couldn't even hear the balls bouncing off of the glass as Malcolm connected over and over again, until the hopper was empty.

"That is so amazing!" said Mikey, struggling to contain his excitement. "Can I try it?"

"Of course," Malcolm replied. "Just make sure you wear the helmet, alright."

"Yes, Sir," answered Mikey.

Malcolm showed Mikey how to reload the hopper and stayed outside with him until he'd gotten the hang of it. In no time, Mikey was bouncing balls off the glass like a pro, as Malcolm and Heidi watched him from inside the house.

"You are amazing with him," said Heidi. "I've never seen him so self-confident, and we have *you* to thank for that."

"He's a bright kid anyway," said Malcolm. "He just needed a chance to prove it to himself."

Mikey continued sending balls into the six-inch-thick, ballistic glass wall, until it was too dark to continue. By the time he came back inside, Malcolm and Heidi had dinner ready, and the three of them ate together in the dining room.

After their meal, Heidi asked Mikey "How would you feel about us moving in here with Malcolm?"

Looking at his mother, Mikey said "I think it would be great, and you won't have to worry anymore because we'll be safe, and nobody can hurt us here."

Malcolm saw the look Heidi shot at Mikey, when he mentioned someone hurting them, but decided not to dig deeper until he could discuss it with her alone. Later that night after Mikey was asleep, Malcolm asked her, "Has someone been threatening you and Mikey, Sweetheart?"

"Not really," she answered. "It's just the guy we rent the house from. Since my ex-husband left, he keeps coming around and showing up at odd hours, asking strange questions and stuff. I try to be nice to him, but I don't want him to think I'm leading him on or anything. One time, when I left to go shopping, I couldn't shake the feeling that he'd been in the house, going through my things while I was gone. When I confronted him about it, He pushed me down on the floor and I thought he was going to hurt me until Mikey started screaming at him. Since then, Mikey refuses to leave me in the house alone, because he's afraid the landlord will come there to hurt me while he's gone."

Malcolm listened without interrupting as she explained what had happened. Afterwards, he said "How about we have all of your things moved over here on Monday afternoon? That way, you can give him notice on the first of the month, and you'll never have to deal with him again."

Smiling, Heidi said "That would be great! I'm so tired of him hitting on me every time he shows up to collect the rent payments. It's like he thinks he can trick me or coerce me into sleeping with him, no matter how many times I tell him it's not going to happen."

Looking into his eyes, she said "I love you, Malcolm. I don't want to live anywhere that you don't, and that has nothing to do with my landlord, or anything else. You make me happier than I can ever remember being, and the way Mikey looks up to you, just amazes me. I keep wondering if I'm going to wake up to find it was all just a dream, because if it is, I want to sleep forever with you."

Without a word, Malcolm took her hand and led her down the stairs to the master suite at the opposite end of the hallway from Mikey's room, and closed the door. Standing behind her, he undressed her before laying her gently on the bed. After undressing himself, he laid down beside her, where their bodies and souls intertwined like ivy; nearly indistinguishable from one another.

Chapter Eleven

Malcolm drove Heidi and Mikey back to their house on Sunday afternoon, with a bundle of packing boxes in the back of his truck. There wasn't a lot for them to pack, and other than their clothes, some kitchenware, and a few personal items, nearly everything could be moved into a storage facility.

The moving truck Malcolm had ordered, showed up promptly at 8:00 a.m., and within two hours, everything was loaded up, and on its way to the storage facility. Heidi left an envelope on the door informing her landlord, Randall McCoy, that the property had been vacated, and that he could keep the security deposit as her final month's rent. She also mentioned that he could come to her place of employment, should there be any remaining questions, and included the address and phone number of the shop.

Shortly after noon, Mr. McCoy came through the front door where he was greeted by Malcolm, who said "Good afternoon, sir. What can I fix for you today?"

"Actually, I'm looking for Heidi Anderson. She left me a message saying she works here now," said Mr. McCoy.

"Hold on just a moment, and I'll get her for you," said Malcolm.

He disappeared into his office and emerged with Heidi a few seconds later.

Upon seeing her, Mr. McCoy launched into a tirade, pointing his finger, and walking toward her as she approached, saying "Who the hell do you think you are? You can't just up and leave without giving me any notice!"

Before he could get any closer, Malcolm stepped in front of Heidi, shielding her from him.

"Hey, asshole!" shouted Mr. McCoy, looking at Malcolm. "This is between her and me, so you need to step aside and mind your own business!"

Malcolm didn't budge, and when Randall tried to push him aside, Malcolm grabbed his wrist with his right hand and placed his left hand against the back of his shoulder. Using the man's own momentum, Malcolm forced him face-first onto the surface of his heavy wooden workbench, holding him firmly in place.

"Let's begin again, shall we?" said Malcolm, quite calmly. "My name is Mr. Abernathy, and I own this shop. That means, I decide who is welcome here, and who is not."

As Randall struggled in vain to free himself, he said "If you know what's good for you, you'll let go of me, right now!"

"Right now, I'm more concerned about what's good for Mrs. Anderson, and you are making that decision an easy one," said Malcolm, unimpressed by the empty threat.

"That bitch owes me money, and she isn't going anywhere until I get it!" said Mr. McCoy angrily. "She can't just up and leave when she feels like it!"

"Actually, she can," stated Malcolm. "Based on the rental agreement, on page two, paragraph four, subsection one, the tenant must provide the owner thirty days' notice or forfeit the security deposit, which is equal to, but not greater than one month's rental fee."

Sensing Randall's waning resistance, Malcolm released him, politely adding "Mrs. Anderson has simply decided to let you keep the security deposit in lieu of paying you the final month's rent."

Upon being released, Randall attempted to regain a modicum of dignity, which was nearly impossible after having been face-planted by Malcolm. Inside, he was seething but realized quickly that any attempt to get past Malcolm would not end well for him.

"What are you, her lawyer or something?" spat out Randall, angrily. "She can't hide behind you forever."

"As far as I'm concerned, she can," stated Malcolm. "Besides, her business with you is obviously complete by both the spirit and the letter of the law, so there's no reason she should ever need to deal with you again," After pausing to watch Randall struggle for the right response, Malcolm added "So, if there's nothing else, I'd suggest you be on your way."

Randall realized he'd been outplayed and backed away toward the front door. "You don't know the can of shit you just opened, mister," he said. "You're going to regret the day you ever laid your hands on me."

"I already do," said Malcolm. "but it's nothing a bit of soap and water won't take care of." Tipping his hat, he added "Good day, sir."

After Mr. McCoy stormed out of the store, Malcolm turned to find Heidi smiling ear-to-ear. "Who are you, Mr. Abernathy?" she asked, walking toward him with a slightly exaggerated hip-swing. "I'm starting to think I've bagged a superhero."

"I am what I've been since the day you and Mikey walked into my life... Yours," said Malcolm, taking her into his arms and kissing her.

Later, as they got back to work clearing Malcolm's list of repairs, Randall McCoy was still fuming. During the incident inside the shop, there had been no witnesses other than the three of them. He could have just let it go and the entire matter would have evaporated into thin air; however, foolish pride often defies logic. Malcolm had made him look like an idiot in front of the woman he'd been trying to seduce for months.

With his family's substantial influence and resources, Randall had grown accustomed to having whatever and whoever he wanted, and rejection wasn't something he'd had to deal with often, if ever. Just because he'd been caught off-guard by some carnival barker once, didn't mean he was going to just let the matter go.

In Randall's mind, there was an implied respect that was due him, and Mr. Fisticuffs had crossed the line. Of course, he didn't want to sully himself with the beat-down he felt was in order for Mr. Abernathy. He had "people" who handled that kind of dirty work for him. Nevertheless, he sure as hell intended to be there when it happened.

After making a few calls, Randall arranged to have some "friends" meet him at Malcolm's shop just before it closed. At 4:40 p.m., they all showed up and gathered across the street at the diner. Twenty minutes later, two armed men came in the front door with Randall, turning the latch and flipping the window sign from OPEN to CLOSED. Another man waited near the side entrance to prevent anyone from slipping out that way.

By the time they entered the building, Malcolm, Heidi, Mikey, and Coco were all inside the office, calmly looking out the window at the men in the shop area. As Randall approached the office, he grabbed the fire-extinguisher near the front counter, and with a galloping start, he tossed it forcefully against the office window.

It thudded against the ballistic glass before falling anti-climactically to the floor without leaving so much as a scratch. Inside the office, Malcolm calmly nodded at Mikey, who clicked on the red dot at the bottom right-hand corner of the monitor screen. Once activated, the security system magnetically locked all of the exit doors and notified the security response agency.

After seeing the fire extinguisher had no effect, one of the men pulled out his handgun and fired it at the glass. The windows, both in Malcolm's home and his shop, weren't only bulletproof—He had personally designed and patented the process for manufacturing them.

The twenty-four layers of tempered glass were sandwiched together around twenty-two layers of thin transparent Kevlar® in alternating fashion. The interior of the windows contained a one-inch airspace filled with ballistic gel that absorbs the kinetic energy of a projectile and distributes it evenly across the entire surface of the window. The result is an impenetrable, soundproof barrier against which, bullets literally flatten and fall to the ground without leaving so much as a blemish on the glass.

Realizing they were as close to their intended targets as they were ever going to get, they tried to make a hasty retreat only to discover the security response team and the Sherriff's department were already pulling up outside the shop, and had taken the man covering the side entrance into custody. Furthermore, the magnetic locks on the exit doors made it impossible for those inside to leave the building.

Before the men could cause any damage by firing into the windows and doors, or other items inside the shop, Malcolm activated the carbon dioxide fire suppression system which instantly flushed the oxygen outside the office from the building through ceiling vents. Within fifteen seconds, all of the intruders in the shop were unconscious and lying on the floor. Once they'd been incapacitated, Malcolm opened the air vents, flooding the facility with oxygen and flushing out the remaining carbon dioxide, before unlocking the doors. Seconds later, the security response team and Sherriff's deputies entered the building and took the intruders into custody.

The entire siege lasted fewer than five minutes while Malcolm and his loved ones watched from the safety of the impenetrable office. By the time the intruders regained consciousness, they were already in custody and the video footage of their assault had been forwarded to the Sherriff's office.

Even though they had to hang around the shop to give their statements to the arresting officers, by 7:00 p.m. they were pulling into the garage at Malcolm's house—A place they all could now call home.

Chapter Twelve

By the time Christmas Eve arrived; Malcolm had repaired every item on his "fix it" list. From a twenty-year-old gas powered go kart, to an eight-millimeter film projector, Malcolm seemed to have the tools and aptitude required to fix nearly anything.

With his workbench cleared, Malcolm was considering closing up and getting an early start on Christmas when a young man entered the shop.

Greeting him at the door, Heidi said "Welcome to I FIX BROKEN THINGS. What can we fix for you today?"

The young man seemed to be in a rush and was carrying a large item packed in bubble-wrap. Setting it down on the counter, he said "I know it's late, but I just got in from Okinawa."

Malcolm approached as he removed the protective wrapping to reveal a pachinko machine. "My kids don't know I'll be home for Christmas, and I wanted to surprise them with this," explained the airman. "It needs a bit of work, and I thought I'd be back in time to have someone repair it for me, but my flight got in a day later than I expected."

Pachinko machines, while extremely popular in Japan, aren't nearly as common in North America. In the United States, most of the places selling and servicing them are located in California, and clearly there wouldn't be enough time to take it there for the repairs it needed.

"A friend of mine from the base, told me about you guys," said the young man. "He said, if any place could get it working again, it would be here."

Looking at Malcolm, Heidi asked "So, what do you think, Mr. Abernathy? Care to take a look?"

Smiling, Malcolm answered "Just try to stop me," as he carried it over to his workbench. Placing it upright on the tabletop, he invited the young man to take a seat while he checked it out.

"What's your name, sir?" asked Malcolm.

"My name's Daniel," the man replied. "I've been traveling for three days, dealing with overbooked flights and longer-than-normal layovers. I really appreciate you helping me out here, Mr. Abernathy."

"Well, unless everything goes awry, I should have it working like a charm in time for you to get home to your family," said Malcolm.

Opening the back of the machine, he used a shop-vac to remove the dust and debris which had accumulated over time. The action was a bit too soft, so he replaced the spring on the flipper and fabricated a new felt bumper pad. Next, he removed the Japanese one-hundred-volt power converter and replaced it with a US one-hundred-ten-volt model. He plugged it in to make sure all the lights were working and discovered a couple of loose connections which he quickly soldered back into place.

After completing the basic maintenance of the machine, Malcolm added a handful of pachinko balls to the upper feeder, expecting them to filter down the wire tube into the launch tray. They didn't. Something was blocking the enclosed aluminum portion of the feeder tube, preventing the chrome-plated steel balls from passing through. He removed the tube and used the eraser end of a pencil to dislodge the obstruction. It was a golden pachinko ball.

"What have we here?" asked Malcolm, picking up the ball.

While golden balls aren't uncommon in pachinko parlors, this one was unusual. Under closer scrutiny, Malcolm determined it wasn't a pachinko ball at all. It was too large and too heavy and bore some kind of inscription in Japanese.

"Hold on just a second," said Malcolm. "I want to check something out," In his office, he tested it with a magnetic screwdriver, then performed acid and density tests which revealed the object was made of solid twenty-four-karat gold.

A few minutes later, he returned to the workbench and asked, "How much did you pay for this machine?"

"With the currency exchange rate, it came to about one hundred fifty bucks," answered Daniel. "I probably overpaid for it, but I wanted to bring my kids something authentic from Japan," he added.

"Well, you certainly picked a winner," said Malcolm, sitting down to re-attach the feeder tube. "The machine, itself, is in excellent condition, and that little obstruction in the feeder tube is worth more than you paid for the entire machine."

"Are you serious?" asked Daniel, excitedly.

"Absolutely," said Malcolm. "The machine is worth at least what you paid for it, and this," said Malcolm, placing the golden ball on the table inside a small Ziploc® jewelry bag "is almost seven grams of solid gold, with a current market value of about three-hundred dollars."

Daniel seemed to snap out of his jet-lagged fatigue as a giant smile appeared on his face. "You've got to be kidding me!" he said loudly. "Are you sure about that?"

"I am," said Malcolm. "I did magnetic, acid, and density tests on it, and it all checks out as solid gold. I have no idea how it found its way into the pachinko tray, or even what its significance is, but since it's only marginally larger than a real pachinko ball, it could have been mistakenly dropped into the hopper by someone who thought it belonged there. There's an inscription on it, but I don't read Japanese, so I'm not sure what it says."

From across the room, Heidi said "I can read Japanese."

Malcolm looked at her curiously as she made her way over to his workbench, saying "You speak Japanese?"

Stopping across the table from him, she held out one hand while standing there with the other hand on her hip. "Let me see it," she said.

"Now, who's the one with tricks up their sleeve?" asked Malcolm with a smile as he handed the little bag to her.

Winking at him, she held the golden ball under the large magnifying glass mounted on his workbench. With a smile, she said "This is the Japanese symbol for love."

Tossing his head back, Daniel said "This is amazing! I was hoping I'd have time to get my wife a Christmas present, but now it seems I've already got the perfect one!" Looking across the table at Malcolm, he added "Everyone told me I should come here. Some even say there's something magic about this place."

"I just fix broken things," said Malcolm. "The magic comes from the love that made you do everything possible to get home to your family for Christmas. Everyone believes in Christmas magic, right?"

Closing the machine, Malcolm tested everything one final time before covering it in the bubble wrap again.

"How much do I owe you?" asked Daniel.

"Parts and labor come to one hundred dollars, and we'll throw in the gift wrapping for you," said Malcolm.

"That sounds more than fair," said Daniel, carrying the machine over to the counter where Heidi was waiting with a smile.

After paying for the repairs, Daniel called an UBER driver while Heidi separately wrapped the pachinko machine and the small ring box she'd used for the golden ball.

When the driver arrived, Daniel thanked Malcolm and Heidi, wishing them a very Merry Christmas as he headed out the door.

Looking at his pocket watch, Malcolm said "It looks like we're going to make it out of here on time tonight,"

Heidi walked up to him and placed her arms around his neck. "You are such a wonderful man," she said. "There really is something magic about you."

With his arms around her waist, Malcolm said "There is magic around us all the time. We just need to pay attention once in a while, so we can see it for what it is."

"But you know so much about so many different things. How can you possibly remember all of that stuff?" asked Heidi, furrowing her brow. "Admit it. You're a warlock, aren't you?"

"I'm whatever you need me to be, Sweetheart," Malcolm answered with a smile. "That's how magic works."

"I'll take your word on that, because since the moment I saw you through the peep-hole, you've been changing the world around me," said Heidi. "I don't care where it comes from. As long as it's a part of you, I'm just gonna go with it."

"Well, let's get this place locked up so we can get started on our Christmas," said Malcolm.

After a final check, Malcolm, Mikey, Heidi, and Coco hopped in the truck, and headed out of the parking lot.

"See you next year!" said Malcolm, waving at the shop as they headed toward the highway and their cozy little log cabin in the woods.

Chapter Thirteen

Christmas and New Year's Eve had never held any kind of special meaning for Malcolm. In fact, during his service as a Navy SEAL, he'd spent most of his holidays in places not even Santa Claus would have dared fly over.

Had someone told him two years ago, that he'd be enjoying this holiday season with his family in the log cabin of his childhood dreams, he'd probably have called them insane. He'd always imagined going down in a blaze of glory on some unnamed patch of sand in the Middle East. It never occurred to him that one day, he would say Merry Christmas and really mean it.

He'd been awake for an hour, laying there in the darkness with Heidi curled up next to him, when she awoke.

"Merry Christmas, Sweetheart," she said, snuggling closer. "Are you ready to play Santa?"

"Santa came and left hours ago," said Malcolm. "He told me the cookies and eggnog you left out for him were fantastic," he added with a chuckle.

"So, you spoke with him," said Heidi, poking him in the ribs. "I didn't hear you get up last night."

"Honey, with my skills, I could sneak into and out of your pajamas without even waking you up," joked Malcolm.

"Now, what fun would that be?" asked Heidi, jokingly.

"Oh my god!" screamed Mikey from the den downstairs. "Mom! Malcolm! You have to see this!" he yelled up the stairway to them.

"Looks like someone beat us to the den." said Malcolm as he and Heidi donned flannel robes and headed down the hallway.

"He sounds like he caught Santa in the act," said Heidi, looking at Malcolm, as he smiled at her suspiciously.

At the bottom of the stairs, Mikey was waiting for them with eyes lit up like the Christmas tree in the corner. Behind him, just in front of the tree, was a dirt bike so new you could still smell the rubber on the tires. Beside it, was an entire compliment of accessories ranging from boots and gloves to a protective jacket and full-face helmet.

Running up to them, Mikey said "You are the best parents ever!" as he wrapped his arms around both of them.

Heidi was speechless, unsure of which part of what was happening, was the most surprising; the motorcycle in the middle of the den, or the fact that Mikey had just used the word "parents". As he rushed back over to the bike, Heidi turned to look at Malcolm, as shocked as Mikey had been.

"Those cookies must have been world class!" said Heidi, wrapping her arms around Malcolm and pressing her head against his chest. "I distinctly remember Mikey asking Santa for a mountain bike,"

"I guess Santa had bigger mountains in mind," answered Malcolm. "Besides, I promised Santa, I'd teach him how and where to ride safely,"

"You'd better; otherwise, I will have to introduce you to Psycho Mom," said Heidi with a sigh.

"Trust me," said Malcolm. "I promise to be a responsible parent,"

"You already are, Baby," said Heidi, squeezing him tightly. "You already are,"

Walking over to the dirt bike, Heidi and Malcolm watched as Mikey excitedly mounted it. Of course, Malcolm had already adjusted it to match Mikey's size, and after trying on everything, he found the safety gear also fit him perfectly.

"When can I ride it?" asked Mikey brimming with excitement.

"After breakfast, we'll take it out behind the house and fire it up," said Malcolm. Pointing toward another box beneath the tree, he asked "Who is that one for?"

Mikey walked over to the box and picked it up before saying, "This one's for Mom!"

"Oh, really?" said Heidi, curiously. Taking the box from Mikey, she was surprised at how light it was in relationship to its size. Upon opening the box, she discovered it was filled to capacity with decorative tissue paper. After removing the paper, she discovered a smaller box taped to the bottom of the large box. "Santa's really making me work for this one,"

"Do you need some help?" asked Malcolm.

"I think I can manage," replied Heidi, removing the smaller box, and tearing into the wrapping paper concealing its contents. Inside was a jewelry box which she slowly opened. "Oh my god!" she exclaimed as the diamond pendant came into view.

Her cheeks were glowing when she looked up at Malcolm, who was smiling from ear to ear. "Do you like it?" he asked?

"You silly, silly man," she replied. "I love it!"

"Let me help you put it on," Malcolm said, opening the clasp and walking around behind her. After hooking the clasp on the platinum chain, he stepped back as she turned to face him.

"It's beautiful," she said. "You are just too much!"

"Wait," said Malcolm. "there's more," Turning to Mikey, he pulled a box from the pocket of his robe and opened it. Inside, was a silver men's bracelet. As Mikey took the box from him, he said "Mikey, I'd like permission to ask your mom to marry me,"

Looking up, Mikey remained silent as he approached Malcolm and wrapped his arms around him. Without a word, he nodded affirmatively, giving his blessing.

Malcolm took the bracelet from the box and attached it to Mikey's wrist, hugging him again. Afterwards, he turned to face Heidi, removing another box from his pocket. There were tears streaming down her cheeks, but her smile revealed the inner joy she felt as Malcolm knelt in front of her and opened the box containing a sparkling princess-cut diamond engagement ring.

"Heidi, I love you and Mikey more than I ever thought I could love anyone. Will you accept me into your lives, and marry me?"

"Yes, yes, yes!" she squealed. "A thousand times, yes!"

Still kneeling before her, Malcolm placed the ring on her finger, then stood and took Heidi into his arms kissing her. A few seconds later, they opened the embrace to include Mikey in the new family circle.

"We didn't forget about you, Malcolm," said Heidi, as Mikey stood next to her, smiling. "We thought it would be harder to find something for a man who has literally everything,"

"Until we realized that Mom had hijacked Coco," said Mikey. "Since, it's impossible to hide anything around you, we had to be creative," he added as Heidi handed him her smartphone.

On the screen, there was a live video feed which showed a Cane Corso puppy wearing a red and green bow around its neck. "He's still at the adoption agency, and we can pick him up later today," said Heidi. "Somehow, I think he'll fit right in with us,"

Looking at the little puppy sleeping peacefully, Malcolm had to smile, saying "He's perfect! Thank you both,"

"Merry Christmas!" said Heidi and Mikey simultaneously before they all headed upstairs to the kitchen.

"Looks like we'll have a full day ahead of us," said Malcolm. "I should have noticed that some of those doggy toys were a bit too large for Coco," he added, acknowledging that their head-fake had successfully thrown him off the scent.

After breakfast, they all piled into Malcolm's truck and drove over to the adoption center to pick up the puppy. He seemed to be expecting them when they arrived, and eagerly trotted out of the building with them at the end of his shiny new leash. By the time they made it back to the house, even Coco couldn't help but love him.

While Malcolm explained the basics of Mikey's new dirt bike to him, the puppy watched them through the window, wondering how he could get out there to investigate.

Mikey had been riding a bicycle for years, so the fundamentals of a two-wheeled vehicle were already seated with him. Malcolm installed a governor on the bike to limit the speed and acceleration until Mikey was more familiar with it, but after only a couple of hours, he was riding around the driveway with confidence. Once the snow melted, they would expand the riding area, but for now, the driveway would have to suffice.

"There is a tracking device on the bike right here, with a crash alert," explained Malcolm. "It'll allow your mother and I to find you, should you get lost or have a spill somewhere. If it's something minor, just pick up the bike and hold this button until the yellow light turns green again, and it'll reset. However, if it stays yellow for longer than one minute, it'll turn red and I **will** be on my way to you, wherever you are, okay?"

"Yes, sir," said Mikey. "I've got it."

"Then go ahead and get some practice in but stick to the driveway around the house," said Malcolm.

"Okay." said Mikey before carefully pulling away.

Inside, Heidi had watched nervously as Malcolm patiently instructed Mikey and was admittedly surprised to see how quickly he'd caught on. When Malcolm came inside, she was smiling as she said "You are a natural. The way Mikey listens to and learns from you is amazing. Even his real father couldn't get through to him the way you do."

"He's a smart young man," Malcolm replied. "All it takes is a little patience and willingness to explain things. Once he gets it, he's got it for good."

"He trusts you," said Heidi. "You are the dad he always needed, but never had."

"And I will always be here for him," said Malcolm. "Come rain or shine."

"Now, if you're half as good with puppies as you are with teenage boys, Malcolm Junior over there should be potty trained in no time flat," said Heidi, looking across the den at Coco and the puppy sleeping peacefully on the hearth near the fireplace.

"Malcolm Junior, huh?" queried Malcolm with a smile. "We'll have to work on a proper name for him, so we don't both come running at the same time when you call one of us."

Hugging Heidi tightly, Malcolm looked around, drinking in the magic of the most wonderful Christmas he could ever have wished for.

Chapter Fourteen

After spending New Years' Eve in Boise, Heidi Anderson became Heidi Abernathy on January first, walking down the aisle with her son, Mikey, just minutes after the city's firework grand finale. They spent the remainder of the week there, enjoying the amenities and activities offered by a city much larger than Mountain Home. Nevertheless, they were glad to be home and anxious to get started on their new lives together.

Returning to work was especially exciting for all of them after such a successful holiday season. I FIX BROKEN THINGS was no longer just an enigma on Main Street, but rather an established part of the Mountain Home community. In fact, the shop's reputation had expanded beyond local boundaries with clients sending in items for repair from cities all over the country.

While most people in Mountain Home felt fortunate to have such a unique shop there, others weren't as enthusiastic about it. More precisely, they were confounded by their inability to assert any kind of leverage over Malcolm's business. This presented a rather unique problem for the small-town mobsters trying to capitalize on the shop's success.

There were no supply lines to interrupt or added fees they could apply to skim a percentage of Malcolm's net profits. After their embarrassing failures at extortion and intimidation, the head of the local crime syndicate was growing more and more impatient. He felt that any company experiencing that type of financial growth should either be subject to his mob tariffs or shut down completely and run out of town.

When Malcolm made the decision to live in Mountain Home, he was hoping to meld with the community and live in virtual obscurity there in small-town USA. Even so, he was never complacent about the caliphate's bounty which would follow him for the rest of his life.

Having spent the majority of his adult life, getting into places specifically designed to keep people like him out, he was uniquely qualified in designing security measures and systems. His primary mandate was to prevent himself from being able to break into it.

He would design a virtually impenetrable barrier, then spend months trying to get around it. Once he did—and he always did—he would spend months reinforcing the points of vulnerability before attempting to bypass them yet again.

The system protecting both his home and business had taken a decade to design and perfect. It was deployed in some of the most secure environments on the planet and was the primary source of his significant wealth. While the core of the system was somewhat standardized, there were always unique attributes custom tailored to each individual site, and only used once.

Of all the security systems he'd designed, only one of the outer perimeters had ever been breached;

and it had been breached by Malcolm, himself. None of the inner vaults, such as those protecting the office in his shop and the entire second floor of his house, had ever been penetrated.

Before opening his business, he'd spent months securing and reinforcing it, working after business hours when no one would notice the massive undertaking happening right next door to them. While he could have easily prevented Randall McCoy and his cronies from even entering his shop, he wanted to make it clear just how futile such an attempt would be. After all, futility is the greatest deterrent known to man.

The reason behind using Randall McCoy to make this very clear statement, was also a calculated one. Not only was he a sexual predator, he was also the son of Earnest McCoy—the same boss referred to by the thugs who'd been waiting outside Malcolm's shop the day after Thanksgiving. While it wasn't Malcolm's intention to provoke further confrontations, he wanted to make it unmistakably clear that he would not be intimidated by anyone.

Of course, Earnest McCoy didn't necessarily agree with that assessment, nor did it sit well with him that he'd been unable to recoup the half-million dollars confiscated by the police from his now deceased former employee during a routine traffic stop. Malcolm Abernathy seemed to be at the very center of the turmoil surrounding McCoy's criminal enterprises, and that was not a condition he would allow to persist.

Having spent the holiday season in an Elmore County detention center, Randall McCoy had his own reasons for wanting Malcolm's business reduced to rubble. While he and one of his gorillas had been released on bail by a very sympathetic judge, the man who'd discharged his weapon inside the shop had been remanded in custody pending his trial.

After years of running rough shod over the law, the sense of entitlement held by the McCoy family had suffered serious damage which needed to be addressed quickly in order to restore their iron-fisted reputation. Ignoring such defiance would be like blood in the water, emboldening others to resist their extortion tactics.

The small-town mob's concerns were happening at an altitude so far beneath Malcolm's radar that he'd seen no reason to take them too seriously. Of course, he'd remain vigilant in protecting his family, but his already heightened sense of awareness and defensive preparations were more than capable of thwarting anything they could throw at him. Should that change, he would adapt accordingly.

By late Spring, business was booming to the point where Malcolm, as fast as he worked, was unable to meet his established turn-around deadlines. It was time to add another repair technician to his team and expand the actual workspace inside the shop. It took a flurry of online job postings and a dozen employment ads in the local newspaper before the right person answered the call.

His name was Jupiter Reynolds, and if ever there had been a jack of all trades capable of matching Malcolm's pace and abilities, it was Jupiter.

He came into the shop after Malcolm had been searching for weeks. Even though his thoughts seemed scattered during the telephone interview, Malcolm seemed to get him, and met him with a smile as he walked through the door.

"Hello, Mr. Reynolds," said Malcolm. "Welcome to I FIX BROKEN THINGS,"

"Glad to be here, Mr. Abernathy," he answered. "I really appreciate the invitation."

"Please. Have a seat," said Malcolm. "Would you like some water, or coffee or..."

"Coffee would be great," said Mr. Reynolds. "I drink it all day long, and still sleep like a baby every night."

As if on cue, Heidi placed a mug in front of him and filled it with the fresh brew. "Cream and sugar?" she asked.

"No. Thank you, Ma'am," he answered with a smile. "I've been drinking it black since I was ten years old."

"As you wish," replied Heidi, filling his cup before returning to the check-in counter.

"So, how did you get into the repair business?" asked Malcolm.

Noticing the electric motor on the table in front of Malcolm, he asked "May I?"

"Be my guest." replied Malcolm, sliding the motor across the table to Mr. Reynolds.

"I worked in my dad's hardware store all through high school," said Mr. Reynolds as he disassembled the motor using the tools Malcolm had on his workbench. "The store was back up in the sticks, so far away from everything, we would always try to fix defective parts and products on location first."

As he continued to speak, he quickly disassembled the motor while answering Malcolm's question. "After a few years, I'd seen and repaired nearly everything under the sun. I just seem to have a knack for it."

In no time, he'd broken the motor down, discovered the short in a cable which had been arcing against the side of the metal housing, and repaired it. "After the attacks on the World Trade Center, I joined the Army as a Combat Engineer and volunteered for deployment to Afghanistan. It was strange, because after spending most of my life fixing things, the Army wanted me to blow shit up."

Jupiter checked the key internal points of the motor to make sure there weren't any other issues that could cause problems. Afterwards, he reassembled it and slid it back across the table to Malcolm, saying "Here you go."

When Malcolm plugged it in and flipped the toggle switch, it hummed quietly to life as if it were fresh from the original factory's assembly line. Obviously impressed, Malcolm asked "When can you start, Mr. Reynolds?"

"I just did," he replied. "and please, call me Jupiter."

With a smile and a handshake, Malcolm welcomed his newest employee to the team and showed him around the shop. Following the brief tour, they went into the office to complete the payroll and tax forms and make it official.

While seated in the office across from Malcolm, Jupiter asked "Do they know?"

"Heidi does," said Malcolm. "She knows about the capture and escape, but I've done my best to spare her from the gory details. She doesn't need those nightmares cruising around inside her head."

"When did you recognize me?" asked Jupiter.

"When you sat down across from me at the workbench," Malcolm replied. "I couldn't tell if you'd recognized me or not, so I didn't bring it up."

"Mr. Abernathy, if there is one thing I will never forget, it's the face of the man who freed me from that god forsaken death camp," said Jupiter. "I never got a proper chance to thank you."

"You'd have done the same for me," said Malcolm.

"I can still remember hearing the screams and gunfire from the interrogation room next to my cell," recounted Jupiter. "I thought they were killing you, and that I'd be next. Then the eerie silence before you showed up at my cell with the keys."

Jupiter's eyes drifted off into distant space as he continued. "After you freed me and handed me the keys to let everyone else out of their cells, I wanted to help you, but I'd been there too long. I just didn't have the strength to fight anymore."

"It's alright," said Malcolm. "I was undercover, pretending to be broken. You guys had been starved and tortured for nearly a month before we found you."

"When I saw all those bodies in the corridor, I honestly believed there was a full extraction team out there. I didn't find out it was just you, until we were airlifted back to Ramstein Air Base," Jupiter said. Looking up at Malcolm, he added "You saved us. You saved us all."

"It was a nasty time," said Malcolm. "but I would do it again without hesitation, my friend."

Jupiter started to speak, saying "I owe you..."

"Nothing," interrupted Malcolm. "You owe me nothing. I'm hiring you because you're exceptionally qualified and I need someone who can help me cover the workload." Following a brief pause, he added "I'm glad to have you onboard."

Standing and sliding the completed forms over to Malcolm, Jupiter said, "Thank you. Thank you for everything."

"Well let's get to work then, Newbie," said Malcolm with a big smile. "We've got a lot of broken things out there to fix."

"Indeed, we do," said Jupiter, nodding as he followed Malcolm into the shop.

Chapter Fifteen

With the shop's prominent location, the intriguing business sign above the door, and the excellent customer service critiques they'd been receiving since day one, I FIX BROKEN THINGS was simply the place to go for any and all repairs from Mountain Home to Boise, Idaho. Through Heidi's internet marketing efforts, she'd been able to expand their client base dramatically over the two years since coming onboard.

While it had never been his specific intention to do so, the formerly near-vacant strip mall had begun attracting new merchants hoping to capitalize on the location and customer traffic generated by Malcolm's shop. It was now somewhat of a tourist destination for servicemembers from the air base, as well as for locals in and around Elmore County.

People would often bring in items for repair, then aimlessly wander the maze of shelves while Malcolm and Jupiter worked their magic, bringing long-dead items back to life. While it seldom took them more than an hour to fix anything, people would happily examine the curiosities in the shop for even longer, losing all sense of time as they did.

During business hours, indoor security was handled exclusively by Bandit. The little Cane Corso puppy had grown into a large Cane Corso puppy; primarily from stealing Coco's food after wolfing down his own. Nevertheless, when it came to the shop, he'd grown up tumbling around those aisles filled with oddities and had developed a sense of ownership for everything he'd discovered there. While anyone inside could wander freely and browse as long as they wanted, Bandit was like a nonchalant stalker, surveilling visitors at knee-level through the shelves from two aisles away.

Of course, everyone and everything around Malcolm had skill and purpose, and Bandit was no different. While he was an absolute baby when it came to soaking up and loving attention, his protective nature toward the inner family circle was like the evil alter-ego of a schizophrenic maniac when he sensed any of them were in danger. Malcolm had exercised the same degree of detail when training Bandit, as he had in teaching Mikey to ride his motorcycle. While he was as gentle as a lamb under most circumstances, his nature would turn on a dime when necessary.

One evening while he and Coco were out in the backyard for their final potty break before bedtime, Coco had completed her business and was trotting back toward the house, completely unaware of the coyote that had been stalking her from the cover of the forest. She was near the middle of the yard when the coyote emerged from the underbrush, charging toward her at full speed. Malcolm had been watching from the garage but was too far away to intervene when the vicious animal pounced.

It never made it to Coco.

Bandit intercepted the larger coyote in mid-run, sinking his teeth into the predator's throat and clamping down with all his might. The surprised coyote struggled to break free, but his fate had already been sealed.

As he rolled around on the lawn, twisting and struggling to dislodge the young dog from his jugular, Bandit remained single-mindedly focused, refusing to slacken his grip for even a second as the two of them tumbled around the backyard, slamming into trees and knocking over heavy lawn furniture. After nearly two minutes of thrashing about trying to free himself, the coyote collapsed near the trees at the edge of the lawn. Bandit remained relentlessly attached to its throat and would not let go until Malcolm finally convinced him it was safe to do so.

Later that night at the Mountain Home Veterinary Clinic, Bandit was treated for two cracked ribs and a right shoulder sprain. Malcolm, Heidi, Mikey, and Coco all spent the night in the waiting room, refusing to go anywhere until they could take Bandit home with them.

Less than two weeks later, Bandit was back to picking on Coco and stealing her food again, having completely forgotten the entire incident. Coco, on the other hand, never completely cleaned her dish anymore; always leaving something for Bandit to "steal" after she had finished eating.

Meanwhile, having studied Malcolm and Jupiter for months, Mikey had learned to make simple repairs himself, with his preference being electronic gadgets and devices. He'd actually become quite skilled at diagnosing and fixing them, with only minimal guidance from his two mentors.

Even after more than a year, Mikey loved nothing more than riding his dirt bike, carving paths along the secluded trails surrounding their house. Sometimes, he would be gone for hours, and even though he'd taken the occasional spill, he was never afraid to get back in the saddle and conquer the obstacle that had bested him. In all that time, the crash indicator light on his motorcycle had only seldom been yellow, and even on those rare occasions, it was never for more than a few seconds.

Very often, Bandit would accompany Mikey, chasing the dirt bike through the woods along the many trails crisscrossing their property. It was an excellent exercise regimen for Bandit, who needed those long runs to burn off the abundance of calories he consumed from both his and Coco's food dishes.

As Heidi and Malcolm sat outside one evening enjoying the beautiful late-summer weather, Malcolm's phone buzzed. It was Mikey's crash sensor.

At first, he only paid cursory attention, as this had happened before on occasion. Mikey was a very skilled rider and falling is simply a part of the process to becoming a motocross competitor; something Mikey had often expressed a desire to do.

After a minute, the crash sensor alert went from yellow to red. Thirty seconds later, Malcolm was on the ATV, burning down the trail behind the house guided by the GPS tracker on Mikey's bike. It only took ten minutes to reach Mikey, who was sitting on the ground, leaning back against a tree with a minor sprain to his left ankle. Bandit was right beside him, daring anyone or anything to approach Mikey with ill intentions. As Malcolm rode up on the ATV, Bandit rushed out to meet him, accompanying him the rest of the way back to Mikey.

"Are you alright, son?" asked Malcolm.

"Yeah, Dad, I'm okay," said Mikey. "A buck leapt out in front of me, and I crashed trying to avoid him. I bent the rim of the front tire, so there's no way I could've ridden it back to the house."

"Yeah, it's done for the evening," said Malcolm. "We'll leave it here for tonight and come back in the morning with the trailer to pick it up," Looking at Mikey, he asked "Did you call your mom?"

"Of course," said Mikey. "I could see on my phone that your GPS tracker was headed this way, so I called her first and told her not to worry," Smiling, he added "I told her not to freak out, but sometimes she still thinks I'm just a baby."

"Mikey, you will always be her baby, so you can rest assured she'll be a helicopter mom for a few weeks," said Malcolm with a smile. "Just go with it for a while, at least until that sore ankle mends. I'll talk to her and let her know it's nothing serious. By the time the motocross qualifications come around, she'll be okay with it."

"Thanks, Dad," said Mikey. "I'm sorry I made you guys worry about me."

"I wasn't worried," said Malcolm. "You're a smart young man who knows how to take care of yourself, and I'm very proud of you, Son." Winking, he added "Besides, Bandit was with you. Even grizzly bears give *him* a wide birth."

"True," said Mikey as Malcolm helped him up and onto the back of the ATV.

Bandit led the way back up the trail where Heidi and Coco were anxiously awaiting their arrival at the garage door. A few minutes later, Malcolm, Coco, and Bandit were seated in the ER waiting room while the medics treated Mikey's ankle under Heidi's exceedingly close supervision.

Chapter Sixteen

There are people in this world who simply cannot let things go. They are so preoccupied with the mistakes and transgressions of the past, that their lives have devolved into an inescapable echo chamber. Caught inside a self-manufactured feedback loop, they lose sight of the future because, for them, the past is all-consuming.

The reason Navy SEAL teams operate under a cloud of obscurity is because killing people tends to create those never-ending feedback loops. Even the smallest particle of information in the hands of someone inside the echo chamber provides a thread that they will continue tugging at, in hopes of unraveling the truths they seek.

There are large echo chambers such as the one created by the caliphate who'd put a bounty on Malcolm's head. There are also smaller ones created by people like Earnest and Randall McCoy, who let insignificant perceptions of slight fester inside them until they are literally bathing in their own toxicity.

On rare occasions, individual echo chambers can bleed into each other creating an entirely new one. Malcolm called it the Semtex® effect, where one small detonation triggers an explosion of a much larger proportion when they are combined. While plastic explosives are very stable and can remain dormant for decades, all it takes is a small detonator to release the destructive energy inside them. The only way to avoid that destructive force is to make sure the Semtex® and the detonator never come into contact with one another. Once they do, the resulting explosion is imminent, massive, and unavoidable.

Malcolm's low profile had served him well for over a decade. He was the consummate professional when it came to business relationships, and his personal life occurred inside a near-impenetrable bubble of privacy. While plenty of outsiders knew *of* him, only Heidi and Mikey truly knew his heart. With the sole exception of Jupiter Reynolds, no one in Mountain Home had even the slightest clue regarding the violence of which Malcolm was capable.

For Randall McCoy, I FIX BROKEN THINGS was a constant reminder of his inability to close the deal. It was the first business, people noticed when heading into the Heart of Mountain Home, and its location at the town's busiest intersection made it nearly impossible to overlook.

Although the majority of the shops in the strip mall had been vacant for close to ten years, after Malcolm's appearance, it had begun to flourish. By the time the McCoy's came up with the idea of purchasing the property entirely, it had already been sold to a management company based in San Francisco, once again frustrating their efforts to gain leverage over Malcolm and the other shopkeepers leasing space there.

To make matters worse, the previous owner had offered to sell the property to Earnest McCoy for pennies on the dollar; however, he'd refused to even make a bid on it. He arrogantly claimed it would be cheaper to wait and buy it from the bank after it went into foreclosure. It was a gamble in which he'd been hopelessly outplayed.

Now that nearly every available space in the mall had been taken, the McCoy family could only watch from the sidelines as it bloomed into the most profitable commerce center in all of Elmore County. There was even talk of further expansion with ongoing negotiations for the new hub of a leading online product distribution company.

By now, it should have been obvious that the McCoy stronghold on private businesses in Mountain Home was rapidly becoming a relic and would soon be nothing more than a distant memory. Unfortunately, that reality was unable to pierce the wall of noise inside the McCoy echo chamber.

Late one Monday evening, after most of the merchants in the strip mall had been visited by an "insurance" agent offering somewhat dubious protection policies, Malcolm noticed a handful of them had gathered behind the building in the employee parking lot. Visibly shaken, one of the shopkeepers had discovered a handwritten note on her windshield which read, "This could have been a bomb."

Being local entrepreneurs, many of them were well aware of the extortion racket run by the McCoy family over the past twenty years. While they'd hoped to escape this plague after moving their business into the mall, Earnest McCoy obviously intended to perpetuate the racket, regardless of their store location.

On the other hand, several of the mall tenants were new to Mountain Home, having invested their life savings in creating livelihoods for themselves and their families. Being shaken down by McCoy's strongmen placed an unanticipated strain on their businesses, making it much harder for them to earn an honest living. However, refusing to pay the protection insurance could put their families at risk and result in them losing everything.

Malcolm listened closely, attempting to reassure the other merchants, and advising them to stick together. In his experience, giving into the demands of terrorists was never a good idea, and would only embolden them to demand even more.

"But, what can we do, Mr. Abernathy?" asked Sharon, who ran a boutique a few doors down from his shop. "I sell clothing and fashion apparel for a living. The young women working for me are terrified, and I can't guarantee their safety."

"I understand," said Malcolm. "I realize how frightening these threats can be, and no one should ever have to do business under the cloud of potential violence." Taking her hand, he continued saying "Sharon, let me look into it and have a chat with the Sherriff. There *is* a solution, and we'll find it together."

"Thank you, Malcolm," said Sharon. "I know you've been here longer than any of us, so we'll follow your lead; but please be careful. I'd hate for anything to happen to you on account of me."

"I'll be fine, Sharon," said Malcolm. "You just keep selling those beautiful dresses. Otherwise, I'll have to drive Heidi all the way to Boise to do her shopping."

Despite her reservations, Sharon managed a smile before getting into her car while Malcolm opened and held the door for her. "You're a good man, Malcolm. I don't know what we'd do without you," she said before waving and heading out of the parking lot.

As he walked back toward his truck, he noticed Heidi and Mikey were standing near the back of the shop near Mikey's motorcycle. Drawing closer, he noticed Heidi was holding a piece of paper in her hand.

"Mikey found this underneath the front tire of his bike," said Heidi, handing the note to Malcolm.

Unfolding the paper, he looked at the handwritten note that read "This could have been a bomb."

"Mount up and ride straight home, Son," said Malcolm. "We'll be right behind you."

As they followed Mikey home, Malcolm looked over at Heidi, saying "I'll take care of it, Sweetheart."

"I know you will, my love. Just promise me you'll be careful."

"I promise," said Malcolm, already miles down the road in his thoughts.

Back at the house, Heidi prepared Malcolm and Mikey's favorite dinner—meatloaf and mashed potatoes with chef salad and Hawaiian dinner rolls. It was her favorite part of the day when they would all sit down together recalling the events of that day and making plans for the next one. Afterwards, Mikey would clear the table and wipe down the countertops before loading and starting the dishwasher. Once that was done, he would disappear into his room where he'd finish his homework before running simulations for the upcoming motocross qualifications.

Malcom and Heidi were in the den watching television when she asked him, "Do you think they'd actually hurt someone?"

"I think they'll try intimidation first," Malcolm replied. "It defeats their own purpose if they prevent the people they are trying to extort, from being able to earn the money they're hoping to steal."

"But what if they decide to use someone to set an example for the other shopkeepers?" asked Heidi.

"There's only one person they would target for that, and you're married to him," said Malcolm. "That's why I'm going to put a stop to this before it gains any more traction."

"What about the guy who followed us up to the gate this evening?" asked Heidi.

"He'll be the perfect alibi," said Malcolm, watching the man on the security monitor as he sat in his vehicle outside the gate. "What better witness than someone working for the man keeping tabs on you?"

"True," said Heidi. "Should I take him some coffee and dessert?"

"Not yet. We don't want to be too obvious," said Malcolm with a smile. "After I leave, activate level one security. It needs to look like business as usual while I'm gone."

Heidi watched as Malcolm donned his thermal running gear; not because it was cold, but because it completely erased his heat signature, giving him a physical profile the size of a squirrel. The compact night-vision goggles would allow him to see everything, even in near absolute darkness. With the canopy of stars overhead, it would be like working in broad daylight for him.

"You promised you'd always come running right back to me," said Heidi. "I'm expecting you to keep that promise."

Walking up to him, she put her arms around his neck and said, "I love you, Malcolm." After kissing him, she added "He threatened my baby. Now, go shut that bastard down."

Seconds later, Malcolm disappeared through a secret doorway at the back of the closet in the master bedroom. Heidi and Mikey both knew about the panic room and the escape chute that opened up behind the trees fifty yards from the house. It was accessible from every closet on the second floor through a concealed tunnel carved into the granite hillside upon which the house was built. The doors would only open after biometric identification, or upon electronic recognition of Coco's and Bandit's microchips. Once the doors were sealed, it would take a direct hit from a military bunker-buster to crack into it.

Earnest McCoy's ranch was only about five miles from Malcolm's house. He'd cased the property numerous times over the past several months and found the security system to be laughable. The antiquated ground motion detectors, static security cameras, and first-generation body-heat recognition sensors could have been defeated by any third-rate combat gamer using stuff available from the internet. The system's only credible component was the human element, and they were lazy, untrained buffoons who believed three-hundred pounds of cholesterol made them dangerous.

Exiting the tunnel at a brisk jog shortly after 1:00 a.m., it only took Malcolm twenty-five minutes to reach McCoy's outer perimeter. To his great surprise, two of the roving security guards were actually still awake.

From the cover of the tall grass outside the fence-line, he dispatched both of them with tranquilizer darts fired from a rifle similar to a modified paintball gun. They'd be out for an hour and awaken with terrible migraines and no recollection of what happened but wouldn't suffer any permanent damage or memory loss.

Once they were down, he silently approached and removed the tiny darts from their necks and tagged them with post-it notes before moving toward the house. Both of the sloths posted at the front porch were sound asleep, counting on the motion detectors to wake them by activating the perimeter lights and alarm. With the skill of an acupuncture therapist, Malcolm tranquilized them manually using darts from the weapon without even needing to fire it.

After tagging them, Malcolm confiscated the magnetic identification card from one of the worthless security guards, and said "Well, Mr. Paxton, you're about to enter every door in this house tonight."

He entered through the back of the house at the service entrance to the kitchen, leaving an orange post-it note on the door. He left others on the backs of each chair at the dining room table, before moving on to the living room, the library, the den, each guest room, and the garage.

Malcolm saved the master bedroom for last, spending several minutes there before quietly exiting the house, returning Mr. Paxton's magnetic ID card, and making his way back across the property to the outer security perimeter of the ranch. It had only taken ten minutes, start to finish, for him to cover the entire house, and none of the security measures in place had even captured the fact he'd been there.

Thirty-five minutes later, Heidi was tapping quietly on the driver-side window of the SUV parked outside the entry gate to their house. The driver, who had dozed off in the vehicle, awakened with a start to find her smiling at him, holding a piece of chocolate cake on a plate in one hand, and a thermos of hot coffee in the other. Malcolm was standing in front of the vehicle shining a flashlight through the windshield at him.

He instinctively reached for the door handle to open it, but quickly closed it again when he noticed Bandit there, aching to get inside the vehicle with him. Instead, he lowered the window just enough to hear Heidi clearly. "Um... Can I help you?" he asked.

"Would you like some coffee and cake?" asked Heidi. "I feel sort of obligated to treat you as a guest since you're parked on our property."

"Well, factually speaking, I'm outside the gate, so I'm not on your property," said the man; his voice dripping with sarcasm.

"Factually speaking," said Heidi. "The property line starts a quarter mile down that driveway, so you are definitely trespassing. I just wasn't sure whether I should have Malcolm shoot you, or if I should offer you some coffee and cake before asking you to be on your way,"

When he turned his head back toward Malcolm, he noticed the double-barrel shotgun pointed at the windshield. Looking back and forth between the two of them dressed in bathrobes and house slippers, he lowered the glass, saying "Coffee and cake sounds lovely, Mrs. Abernathy," Reaching out the lowered window slowly, he took the plate and the thermos from Heidi, under the watchful eyes of Bandit, who *really* wanted inside that vehicle. "I'll be on my way now. Please pardon the intrusion," he said before starting the vehicle and slowly driving back down the driveway to the public access road.

"Who was that?" asked Mikey as they approached the front door from the driveway.

"Just a man who'd lost his way, Son," replied Malcolm, walking up the stairs with his arm around Heidi. "Nothing your mom's chocolate cake couldn't set straight,"

"Chocolate cake!" exclaimed Mikey. "That sounds like a perfect 3:00 a.m. snack to me,"

"It does, doesn't it?" said Malcolm, as the three of them headed into the kitchen.

Outside, Bandit laid down and waited on the front porch for a while. He *really* wanted to get inside that car!

Chapter Seventeen

At 2:30 a.m., all hell broke loose at the McCoy ranch. The undetected intruder had set the alarm clocks in every room for precisely that time, along with the oven timer, the microwave, and every single television in the house. The rooms were absolutely littered with color-coded post-it notes.

There were pink notes on the pillows beside the heads of everyone who'd been sleeping in the guestrooms, which read "This could have been a bullet," The message on the blue notes placed under every toilet seat in the house, said "Pressure Release Trigger". Yellow notes on the backs of the dining room chairs said "Shrapnel" and the green note inside the fruit basket at the center of the table said, "Improvised Explosive Device,"

On the chest of each security guard was a red sticky-note bearing the word "Sniper" and the orange notes on every exit door from the building said "Claymore".

In the master bedroom, pinned to the pajama shirt Earnest McCoy was wearing, was the note his insurance agent had left beneath the front tire of Mikey's motorcycle. Covering the button on the clock radio beside his bed was a note that said "Dead Man's Switch," and on the pillow beside his head, was a live hand-grenade with a note which read, "Next time, I'll take the pin with me,"

When Earnest McCoy left the master bedroom in a daze, there were green notes spaced every three feet along the floor, and literally dozens of yellow notes covering the walls along the entire length of the hallway.

In the garage, there were blue notes beneath every vehicle, and the tires had all been punctured and deflated using an icepick from the kitchen. Outside, the surveillance cameras had been repositioned and were now facing each other, and the power strip where both the motion sensors and thermal imaging equipment were connected, had simply been unplugged from the wall socket, rendering them useless.

Adding insult to injury, the magazines had been removed from the weapons of every security guard, including their secondary firearms, and placed in the trash can beneath the desk in the library. The handgun fixed to the underside of the desk was still there, but the magazine had been removed and was in the trash can along with all the others. Finally, the painting covering the safe in the library had been taken down and was on the floor leaning against the wall beneath it.

When Earnest McCoy called the man, who'd been observing the Abernathy's house, he was sitting in a convenience store parking lot, drinking hot coffee, and eating the most delicious piece of chocolate cake he'd ever tasted. Nevertheless, he could attest to the fact he hadn't seen anyone leave the property, and all of them had been there since the previous evening.

While Earnest McCoy was nearly climbing the walls, five miles away, Malcolm, Heidi, Mikey, and Coco were sleeping soundly without a care in the world. Bandit remained upstairs watching the front of the house from the sofa beneath the living room window, but the remainder of the night was uneventful.

I FIX BROKEN THINGS opened punctually at 10:00 a.m., with Malcolm and Jupiter working uninterrupted through the entire day. The insurance salesman who'd promised to return for final decisions from the shopkeepers in the strip mall, was conspicuously absent that day. In fact, by Saturday, he still hadn't so much as shown his face at any of the establishments there. Even the diner across the street had been spared his irritating presence.

With no apparent lingering threats, Malcolm and Heidi decided to let Mikey travel with his motocross team to the qualifications in Boise over the weekend. He'd worked harder than everyone else and was, without a doubt, the best rider on the team. He'd earned that weekend in Boise and would be in great hands under supervision of the team's coach, Dallas Burnette.

Coach Burnette had been winning state and national championships for over ten years and respected Mikey's riding skills. He was impressed by the way Mikey studied the tracks, memorizing each course and attacking them aggressively during the race. From the back of the pack, he consistently fought his way to the front, and once he took the lead, he never lost it.

With the number of regional trophies decorating the shelves in his bedroom, even Heidi had to acknowledge the fact that Mikey had grown into a capable young man. Besides, travelling with his friends and colleagues would be an excellent opportunity for him to build camaraderie while spending time with his peers.

After closing up shop for the weekend, Malcolm and Heidi were preparing to leave when a smiling Sharon approached them in the employee parking lot behind the building. Excitedly, she said "Thank you Malcolm. I don't know what you told the Sherriff, but the problem seems to have evaporated into thin air. Not one of the shops have been approached since Monday, and the threats against them seem to have dried up completely,"

"That's great news, Sharon," said Malcolm with a smile. "but I haven't had a chance to speak with the Sherriff yet. Apparently, he's been preoccupied with a break-in out at the McCoy ranch, but he said he would drop by as soon as he was able to get away. Evidently, Earnest McCoy is something of a snowflake when he's on the receiving end of injustice."

"Well, I really don't care why it's been so peaceful, but whoever it was that brought about the change, is my hero," said Sharon. "Hell; if they find out who did it and arrest him, I'll post bail from my own pocket to get him out, and I'm sure I wouldn't be the only one."

"You can add us to that list," said Heidi. "It's about time someone made it clear to those creeps they can't just stomp on the whole town whenever and however they want to."

"I'll certainly let you know if we ever need to pass the hat, but I'm crossing my fingers and hoping we've heard the last of it," Said Sharon, walking back towards her boutique. "Have a nice weekend, you two!"

As Malcolm and Heidi were about to get into their truck and head home, they noticed a man approaching him from the alleyway alongside the building. Malcolm and Bandit recognized him immediately and as he drew nearer, so did Heidi.

"Mr. and Mrs. Abernathy," he said, quite respectfully. "I just wanted to return the plate and thermos you gave me the other night. By the way. The chocolate cake was to die for!"

"Thank you," said Heidi as the man handed the items to Malcolm.

"I also wanted to apologize," said the man, clearly remorseful of the circumstances surrounding their previous encounter. "I honestly had no idea who I'd signed on with prior to that night. I recently retired after twenty-five years with the Boise Metropolitan Police Department and was only looking for a part-time security job. I was so preoccupied with touting my own background and resume, I didn't even think to look into Mr. McCoy's before I took the job."

"It's a common mistake." said Malcolm. "I'm sure we've all been in a similar situation at one time or another."

"Still," said the man. "It's no excuse for spying on decent folks like yourselves; especially, for a man like Earnest McCoy." Offering his hand to Malcolm, he said "I'm very, very sorry."

With a smile, Malcolm shook the man's hand before releasing it so he could also shake Heidi's hand. While Bandit kept him under tight surveillance, he remained calm as the man delivered his apology and turned to walk away.

"Are you still looking for work?" asked Malcolm.

Stopping to look back, the man said, "After twenty-five years of protecting and serving, it's a lot tougher than I imagined, sitting on my ass at home all day." With a perplexed smile, he added "If I don't find something to keep me busy, my wife will probably have me committed, if she doesn't end up killing me herself."

Despite the tension that had been lingering between them, they all had to laugh at what clearly had been the man's motivation for taking the first job that landed in his lap. Even Bandit, sensing the air of relief around them, began wagging his tail.

"What's your name, Sir?" asked Malcolm with a genuine smile.

"Detective... Um, I mean Richard. Richard Dyson," said the man. "Old habits," he added with a chuckle, shaking his head.

"In light of some recent activity around the mall, I think the property management company in San Francisco might be willing to hire some security to keep an eye on the place," said Malcolm. "I'd be happy to put in a good word for you, Mr. Dyson."

"Are you serious?" asked the man, completely astonished.

"Absolutely," said Malcolm. "When I first opened up shop here, it was only me and the bank a few doors down. Now, we've got a full house, and the situation has completely changed. They need to keep pace with the changing times and adding security would be a great place to start."

"Well, if it's a serious offer, then I'm your man," said Mr. Dyson. Thinking about it, he added "It's kind of funny though. I'd be getting paid to watch *you* all over again."

"Me and everyone else in the mall," Malcolm replied. "The difference is that this time, you wouldn't be trespassing."

"A small but consequential distinction," said Mr. Dyson, reaching out to hand Malcolm his business card.

"Then I'll make some phone calls and see if we can put you to work next week," Malcolm replied, accepting the card, and getting into the truck with Bandit and Heidi. Moments later, they were on their way home.

During the drive, Malcolm noticed Heidi kept looking over at him. Curiosity finally got the better of him and he asked, "What?"

"I know you're probably tired of hearing this, but do you even realize how freaking amazing you are?" she asked. "I mean, who else—who else in the world would have offered that guy a job after what happened?"

Shrugging his shoulders, Malcolm said "Sometimes, good people slip into bad situations. I can only imagine how difficult it must have been for him to bring back that thermos and plate."

"No doubt about it," said Heidi. "His wife probably washed them and reminded him to return them to us, and I'm sure he must have wrestled with it for quite a while."

"My thoughts exactly," said Malcolm.

"I don't know how you do it, but you always find new ways to amaze me," Heidi continued. "I swear to God, Malcolm. I love you so much that I just want to crawl inside you, and wear you like a suit sometimes," Pausing for effect, she looked at him and said, "I am so turned on right now, I can't wait to get home, just so you can smash me."

Without warning, the two of them were pressed firmly into the plush leather seats of Malcolm's truck as he floored the gas pedal and the supercharged engine screamed to life. With every cop in the city jumping through hoops five miles away in the opposite direction, the course was clear, and Malcolm was suddenly in a hurry to reach the house.

Chapter Eighteen

The following Monday morning, Malcolm called Mr. Dyson to inform him that he'd been hired. Based on his resume and extensive law enforcement background, it was an easy decision.

Since a single individual wouldn't be able to provide around-the-clock security for the entire mall, the management company also decided to hire five additional security guards. They would be interviewed and vetted by Mr. Dyson, who would serve as the security superintendent.

The last remaining vacancy in the strip mall had remained empty due to its smaller size. It had last been occupied by a legitimate insurance company some twelve years earlier and was the perfect headquarters for the newly authorized security team.

Mr. Dyson reported for work an hour after receiving Malcolm's phone call, and by the end of the day, he'd scheduled interviews with several candidates provided by the Idaho Department of Labor.

In the meantime, Heidi ordered a security vehicle, office furniture and communications equipment, while Malcolm designed a surveillance system to cover every inch of the mall, both inside the shops, and around the perimeter of the building. Each shop would now have the ability to monitor their own individual businesses from anywhere in the world, and the security office could maintain oversight of every shop in the mall using the same software applications, based on the permissions granted by individual shopkeepers.

Within a week, the security office was nicely outfitted, completely staffed with security professionals, and equipped with a state-of-the-art surveillance system. Needless to say, Earnest McCoy's aspirations of keeping the mall's entrepreneurs under his thumb, were officially dead.

On the other hand, Mikey's aspirations for becoming a professional motocross champion were well on their way to reality. During the qualifications in Boise, Dallas Burnette's team had produced three riders who qualified for the finals. While he was the third overall to qualify behind Stacy McNeill and Marcus Williams, Mikey had ridden a flawless race until the whoops section on the very last lap. Somehow, he'd lost his grip on the throttle for a moment which allowed two riders to slip past him on the final hundred yards of the track.

While he'd qualified way ahead of the other riders in his own team, his teammates were somewhat shocked by the apparent amateur mistake. Nevertheless, Mikey was very satisfied with his performance and was looking forward to the upcoming race, even though he wouldn't be starting from the pole position. Malcolm was delighted upon hearing the results, being the only one other than Mikey who understood the tactical importance of coming in third.

Before leaving for the qualifications in Boise, Malcolm had explained to Mikey the psychology of a winner. "Win when it counts," said Malcolm. "The pole position puts a bullseye on your back for everyone behind you. By starting from within striking distance but not at the front of the pack, you can allow everyone else to challenge the leader while you observe their tactics and techniques. By the end of the race, most of them will have eliminated each other in the scramble for first place, leaving you mentally fresh and able to exploit the weaknesses of the remaining riders. By exercising patience, you can emerge from the pack unexpectedly and win when it counts."

Malcolm explained, "The key to victory is to set aside pride and arrogance that only serve as a distraction and do all of your celebrating from the winners circle after the race."

Mikey had fully embraced and executed Malcolm's strategy, holding back, and luring the competition into a false sense of security. As a result, they were completely unaware of Mikey's true skill, giving him enormous tactical and psychological advantages.

On race day, cameras saturated the screens along the packed course with images of the two front runners as each of them submitted to pre-race interviews and photo ops. Mikey received only cursory coverage with no real attention other than the obligatory mentioning of his name during the pre-race lineup. Preceding the race, Mikey and Malcolm exchanged knowing glances before Mikey pulled on his helmet, covering his face and eyes. Moments later, the starting gun fired, and they were off.

As expected, the two front-runners lit up the track right from the start of the race, dazzling the crowd with acrobatic jumps and maneuvers that elicited cheers and applause from the crowded stands. Jake had actually fallen back two places by the time they'd completed the second lap.

Heading into the third lap, Marcus made his move, slipping past Stacy on the inside of the first turn. As the third and fourth positioned riders realized Stacy had lost the inside track, they also slipped past him before he could recover. Near the end of the third lap, Stacy's frustration became evident as he released the throttle too late to navigate the final turn and lost control of the motorcycle, crashing into the barrier on the outside edge of the track.

Realizing his primary rival was out of the race, Marcus was already mentally celebrating, taking the jumps and acrobatics to a whole new level as he prematurely basked in the glory of his imminent victory. In his arrogance, he failed to notice that Mikey had already dispatched the riders in second and third place and was rapidly closing in on Marcus. When they reached the final long jump preceding the final turn, Mikey made his move.

Marcus loved the attention and applause that erupted from the crowd during his high-flying aerial acrobatics, and feeling confident in his victory, his final jump was high and spectacular. As the flashing cameras and cheering spectators lifted Marcus' ego, Mikey accelerated taking the jump at a lower, faster trajectory that allowed his tires to more quickly bite into the dirt and accelerate through the final turn.

For Marcus, the extra second of airtime seemed to take forever while he watched Mikey dive into the curve preceding the final straight away. Although Mikey was now slightly in the lead, Marcus was confident he would hesitate and lose speed on the whoops section preceding the finish line.

He could not have been more wrong as Mikey nailed the throttle, skipping over the series of low bumps as if performing a choreographed dance atop their peaks. He crossed the finish line, taking the checkered flag going away, nearly two full bike lengths ahead of Marcus as the crowd went absolutely wild. Mikey had won the race only a fraction of a second behind the track's best time ever, set by his coach, Dallas Burnette.

As the network television team in the press box frantically re-worded their commentary to describe a stunning victory literally snatched from thin air, Mikey took his victory lap, executing aerial maneuvers and acrobatics that visually put those of his rivals, Stacy McNeill and Marcus Williams, to shame.

Heidi and Malcolm joined Mikey in the winners' circle, where for the first time, he became the center of attention framed by the glowing faces of his parents and the other members of his motocross team. The previously unheralded rider from Mountain Home had taken the motocross world by surprise with his stunning victory at the Idaho state championship. Mikey's victory had automatically qualified him for the national motocross championship competition, and it seemed everyone wanted a piece of him.

It's amazing how quickly a local pastime can lead to national and international recognition. For a teenage boy who could ride like an animal, fearlessly eliminating the competition while remaining emotionally grounded, Mikey was marketing gold. Even so, he never let the celebrity of his victory overshadow the hard work required to win at the national level.

Mikey rode every day, and studied the course incessantly using the virtual reality software on his gaming console. After creating a digital replica of the course, he could study every minute aspect of it in great detail, and as the competition drew nearer his focus on the race was laser-like.

While motocross racing at the local level garners very little outside attention, once a rider has won regional and state competitions, their race footage is viewed by enthusiasts from all over the world. In some cases, the performances of individual racers are even recreated in digital form for use on gaming platforms.

For all of our faults and differences as human beings, our hobbies and pastimes are often shared, even among our adversaries. While our social, political, and ideological differences may make us enemies, watching the gravity-defying aerial acrobatics of a motocross champion provides a thrill which can easily be appreciated despite our other, more polarizing opinions of one another.

In Riyadh, Saudi Arabia, Kareem Abdul Amari was an extreme example of this personal paradox.

While watching motocross newsreels and the rider highlights from the victory lap after the Idaho state championship in Boise, he was in awe of Mikey's racing skills. The way Mikey laid in wait, stalking the leader until the last possible instant, and then stealing victory from him, even though it was within his grasp, was masterful.

He'd watched the highlights of the race dozens of times before finally viewing the actual trophy presentation. In a short, three-second clip of Mikey and his parents, Kareem's admiration for Mikey was suddenly counterbalanced by rage upon recognition of the man standing behind him. Just as Jupiter Reynolds could never forget the face of the man who'd saved him, Kareem Abdul Amari would never forget the face of the man who had killed both of his older brothers and his uncle.

He had been watching the video clips for weeks, attempting to understand the complexity of Mikey's riding style. It was aggressive but not overt, skillful but not flashy, and strategically brilliant from the starting gate through the finish line. While the other riders were playing checkers, Mikey was playing three-dimensional chess without even a hint of arrogance. He'd sat in the midst of friends who shared his admiration of Mikey's skills, professing him to be possibly the greatest motocross rider of all time.

Now, he was forced to face a painful reality, sandwiched between his idol and his archenemy. Thanks to a three-second moment captured in time, he knew where to find **both** of them.

Chapter Nineteen

As individuals, we are faced with a plethora of decisions each day, beginning the very moment we open our eyes and decide to get out of bed. While our decisions can be influenced by external factors, responsibility for the actions we take based on those decisions, is our own to bear.

Nearly eight-thousand miles east of Mountain Home, a young man sat sipping coffee on the patio outside his home, as the sun climbed slowly into the sky over Saudi Arabia. For days he'd been wrestling with options and asking Allah for guidance, yet he seemed no closer to enlightenment that morning than he had been in the days preceding it.

When his brothers began immersing themselves in the politics of hate and intolerance, Kareem had encouraged them to embrace mankind's diversity through the peaceful teachings of Islam. He stood against the distortion of his peaceful religion into the basis for their senseless acts of violence. Still, they were his brothers, and it was easy for him to be swept up in his family's cries for revenge while suffering from the pain of a broken heart.

His father was crushed after learning he'd lost his brother and both of his eldest sons in a single incident, saying "No father should outlive his children." Even as he lay dying, he'd summoned Kareem to his death bed, hoping to pass the legacy of revenge on to him; however, he expired only minutes before Kareem could reach his bedside.

For many of his extended family members, the understanding that Kareem must now bear the mantle of the avenging son, was implicit. While it is easy to hate the face of the anonymous man who killed your radicalized family members and overlook the circumstances that put them all in that situation to begin with, at some point, truth must prevail over rhetoric.

Only a few weeks earlier, Kareem Abdul Amari would have flown to the United States simply to witness his favorite motocross superstar in action during the upcoming national finals. Now he was torn between his genuine admiration for Mikey and the superimposed, externally perpetuated hate which could only be satisfied by spilling the blood of his father.

Having already purchased tickets for both the flight and the national championship competition hours earlier, Kareem would definitely be flying to the United States in mid-August. The one remaining question in *his* mind would also be asked when he presented his visa at the customs and border security checkpoint inside the airport. "Is your trip to the United States for business or for pleasure?"

In Mountain Home, Idaho, shortly before midnight, Malcolm received a one-word text message from a blocked number, which read "Armadillo." Sitting up on the side of the bed, he responded with the word "Zipper" before silencing his phone and spooning himself back in behind Heidi, wrapping his arms around her.

"Who was that?" asked Heidi.

"It was my secret lover?" answered Malcolm, feigning a yawn.

Jabbing him with her elbow, she said "Stop lying. You know that nobody wants you but me."

Laughing and squeezing her tightly, he replied "I hope you're right about that."

She knew he was trying to distract her by changing the subject. His phone never rang or received any alerts after 11:00 p.m. and the mere fact that it had, was reason enough to raise her concerns for him.

"Malcolm," she said in a calm but serious tone. "Talk to me Baby."

Following a long period of silence, Malcolm said "A close relative of one of the men who held me captive near Damascus just purchased airline tickets for travel to the United States."

"Are we in danger?" asked Heidi.

"No," answered Malcolm without hesitation. "But I will find out more in the morning. We've scheduled an encrypted call for 6:00 a.m. and as soon as I know more, you'll be the second person to know about it."

Without another word, both Malcolm and Heidi drifted off to a deep, regenerative sleep.

The next morning, just as Malcolm and Jupiter were about to get started on their relatively light workload, Mr. Dyson called from the security office. One of the electrical outlets mounted near the ceiling to accommodate a wall-mounted television, wasn't working, and he wondered if either Malcolm or Jupiter could take a look at it before calling in an electrician.

Jupiter volunteered. He hadn't seen the new security office and was anxious to check it out. Grabbing his electrical tool kit, he headed over to the office where Mr. Dyson met him at the door.

"Good morning, Jupiter," said Richard. "Thanks for coming over to take a look."

"Hey, Richard," answered Jupiter. "I've been wanting to check out your office anyway." Looking around, he added "Wow! You have quite an operation going on here."

"Yeah, that Malcolm designed a doozey for us," said Richard with a smile. "It's the best mall security system I've ever seen, and while working for Boise MPD, I saw a truckload of them over the years."

"Malcolm is a different kind of animal," said Jupiter with a smile as he climbed a ladder to reach the defective socket. "There aren't many men like him."

"I agree," said Richard. "but it's tough to get into his head. Even though I feel as if I can absolutely trust him, I really don't know much about him." Explaining further, Richard continued, saying "After working as a detective for so long, I can normally read a person within a few minutes of meeting them, but with Malcolm, I get nothing."

"Malcolm's head is the last place most people would ever want to be," said Jupiter. "Don't get me wrong. He's the kind of man you want in your corner, but heaven help you if he ever come's gunning for you."

"How exactly did you two meet each other?" asked Richard, curiously.

"I was about a day or two away from starving to death, but probably wouldn't have been alive that long anyway," said Jupiter. "Fourteen ISIL guards had been holding us in a prison compound for over a month, beating the shit out of us every single day. By the time they dragged him past our cells into the interrogation room, I'd been beaten so badly that I could only see out of my left eye because the right one was swollen shut."

Richard swallowed hard and listened intently as Jupiter continued.

"They had stripped him down to his briefs and beaten him like a dog, he was covered with bruises and there was a long, deep cut across his chest," said Jupiter. "I'd been in that interrogation room where they would beat on me and kick me in the face right in front of the webcam they had set up. I swear, I thought he was already dead, and they were just dragging him in there to cut his head off for the people watching that damn live feed."

Pausing for a moment, Jupiter's mind had obviously drifted into a very dark place before he snapped out of it and continued. "His hands were cuffed behind his back, and even his feet were bleeding from being dragged across the rocky dirt floor. A few seconds later, the screaming started, and I just knew they were killing him in there and would probably be coming for me next. I mean, after a month, what else would they have kept us alive for, if not for their propaganda videos?"

Jupiter was already replacing the socket cover, having quickly found and repaired the problem as he continued with his recollection of the event. "I remember how all the screaming stopped and the door to the interrogation room opened. I will never forget the sound of the rusted hinges on that door. Every time they opened it, one of us would be dragged into that hellhole and wailed on again. I heard someone outside my cell and thought they'd come to finish me off next, but when I looked up at the man opening the cell door, it was Malcolm."

Looking at Richard, Jupiter said "He was covered in blood from head to toe, but he was speaking to me so calmly, and as he used the key to open my cell door, I noticed his hands were as steady as Death itself. After he freed me, he gave me the keys and I could barely hold onto them because I was shaking so badly."

The look on Jupiter's face was intense as he continued, saying "When I came out of my cell, there were dead people all along the corridor. The rifles were missing from two of the corpses, but three more of them were still draped across the bodies of soldiers who would never use them again. We could hear automatic weapons fire as I opened all the cell doors, and as we made our way down the corridor, we collected guns and ammo from bodies lying on the floor in case we needed them to fight."

"I could see sunlight coming in from under the thick steel-plated door at the end of the corridor and noticed a shadow crossing through it," Jupiter continued. "We all had our weapons trained on that door when I heard Malcolm's voice shouting, telling us he was coming in, and not to shoot. At Malcolm's direction, we all waited inside the doorway until we heard the helicopters overhead. A few seconds later, they landed, and we ran out toward them, expecting to take on enemy fire as we dragged and carried each other across the compound to the helicopters. A Navy SEAL extraction team had set up a perimeter to secure our path to the rescue birds, but not one of them had to fire a single shot. Malcolm had killed everyone."

Jupiter seemed to snap out of a semi-trance as he said, "Once we were airborne, Navy F-18 Hornets came through and laid down a wall of 'kiss my ass' that obliterated every inch of the compound. A few minutes later, we were landing on a carrier and medical crews were taking us off the choppers and into the ship's hospital. When it came to Malcolm, he'd been shot several times and finally passed out during the helicopter ride back to the carrier. When *his* bird landed, every member of that SEAL team laid a hand on his stretcher, and they all carried him inside together."

After plugging in the television, Jupiter climbed back down the ladder and picked up the remote from the countertop. With a tap of the power button, the television immediately came to life. "There you go," said Jupiter, handing the remote back to Richard, before asking "How did you and Malcolm meet?"

"I was working for Earnest McCoy, keeping an eye on him," said Richard. "When I saw him and Heidi walking toward my car, I wasn't sure what to do, so I drew my weapon and put it on my lap, then pretended to be asleep inside the car. I didn't realize that I was on their property even though I was outside the gate, so I thought I'd have been in my rights to defend myself if I needed to. When Heidi tapped on my window, I had a choice; either go for my gun or go for the cake."

"That cake was delicious, wasn't it?" said Jupiter.

"Yes, it was!" said Richard with a grin.

"You made the right choice," said Jupiter, taking his tools and heading toward the door, where he paused. "God had mercy on you that night, because had you touched that gun... Malcolm wouldn't have."

After Jupiter left the office, Richard hit the auto-redial button on his cell phone and called his wife. When she answered, Richard said, "I just called to say I love you, Karen."

"I love you too, Richard," answered Karen. "But what brought *that* on, all of a sudden?"

"Remember how I skipped dessert after dinner on the night I took that first security job in Mountain Home, because I didn't want it to make me too fat, and you told me 'One piece of chocolate cake wouldn't kill me'?" Richard asked.

"Yes," replied Karen. "Why?"

"You were right." said Richard.

Chapter Twenty

Kareem arrived in Las Vegas five days before the motocross championship finals. His large entourage included several family members and friends who had been motocross enthusiasts for many years. There were also a number of individuals accompanying them to provide security for the last living son of a prominent family associated with the Caliphate.

By the time they arrived at McCarran International, Malcolm already knew everyone traveling with the group and the name of the hotel in which they were staying for the duration of their visit. While intelligence agents monitoring the Caliphate, kept a constant eye on everyone associated with them, it was done inconspicuously under numerous layers of discretion.

Although Malcolm was understandably suspicious, it was entirely possible that Kareem Abdul Amari was in the United States solely for the purpose indicated on his customs declaration forms... Pleasure. Furthermore, it wasn't the first time he'd been a spectator at the National Motocross Championship Finals in the United States. In fact, he'd been there four of the past six years and was clearly a huge fan of the sport according to his social media pages.

While Malcolm was somewhat skeptical once he saw the number of comments and posts from Mikey's fan page that had been shared to Kareem's followers; In all honesty, they were the same clips and highlights several of Mikey's fans had shared numerous times among *their* followers as well. Kareem's admiration of Mikey's talent as a rider seemed to be legitimate; however, there were also videos linked to his page in which he swore to find the infidel who killed his brothers and his uncle and to avenge them.

While Malcolm would do everything possible to avoid a deadly confrontation with Kareem and any members of his entourage, if they threatened his family, he would ruthlessly slaughter them all and completely eradicate the threat by eliminating anyone left alive who was capable of carrying it out. That being said, he genuinely hoped Kareem's admiration of Mikey's talent was authentic and saw it as a potential point for a meeting of their minds.

Mikey travelled to Las Vegas with Malcolm and Heidi two days before the event, giving them time to get settled and take in some of the tourist attractions while Mikey went through his race preparations with Coach Burnette. The security at the track was tight, primarily because the network covering the event didn't want the details of it leaking out before the gates opened on Saturday afternoon. While the individual riders were allowed to walk the course, even they wouldn't be permitted to ride on it prior to the day of the race.

Since many of the competitors in the race were under the age of twenty-one, the coaches preferred accommodations that were closer to the track than they were to Las Vegas Boulevard. This would give them access to the track without having to contend with the distractions associated with mega-casino hotels located on the strip. Since the rooms for Mikey's team were all reserved under the coach's name, the individual racers could avoid the crush of fans that would invariably pop up, hoping to catch a glimpse of their favorite rider, and possibly even get a photo with, or an autograph from them.

After walking the course with Coach Burnette, Mikey retired to his room and connected his VR game controller to the television. He modified the virtual track to match the course's actual layout and ran multiple race simulations in order to identify hidden pitfalls and potential ambush points where he could slip past other riders unexpectedly. By the time he fell asleep, he could probably have navigated the course wearing a blindfold.

Since Heidi had never been to Las Vegas, Malcolm gave her the royal treatment, ordering a limousine and taking in one of the most popular production shows on the strip after dinner in one of the city's most exclusive fine dining restaurants. Although they thoroughly enjoyed themselves, Malcolm remained vigilant, keeping an eye on his surroundings while closely monitoring Mikey's GPS location and activity tracker until they returned to the hotel late that evening.

While Kareem and his entourage were saturating themselves with alcohol and enjoying the Las Vegas nightlife, their party was one person short. When a family has that much money, they can make it rain and attract the attention of countless young women hoping to get into their cordoned-off VIP section. Fill that area with gorgeous women and no one will even notice who slips in or out of it during the course of the night.

Amir Haddad had provided personal security and clean-up services for the Amari family for a dozen years. Even before departing Riyadh, he knew where Coach Burnette's team would be sequestered. While he'd been given specific orders by Kareem to observe but not interfere, his personal relationship with Kareem's father had been more influential in shaping his desire for vengeance.

Earlier that day, he observed Coach Burnette entering the track with the members of his racing team and when they left, he was able to confirm that Michael Abernathy was indeed staying in the hotel with the rest of the team. At one point he thought he spotted Malcolm leaving the hotel with Heidi; however, the encounter was so brief that he couldn't be sure. Since Malcolm had the driver drop them off at the rear entrance to the hotel, Amir didn't see them when they returned.

Other than confirming that Mikey was indeed staying with the team at the hotel, Amir's stakeout yielded little if any useful information for Kareem. For Malcolm, it was a completely different story altogether. He spotted Amir outside the track that afternoon, and again when the limousine picked them up at the valet for their evening on the town. When he was still in his vehicle near the hotel upon their return, Malcolm knew they were being surveilled.

Before retiring for the evening, Malcolm and Heidi checked in on Mikey to see how his race preparations were coming along and to remind him that "rest" was also an integral part of that preparation. Taking the hint, Mikey went to bed soon after they'd left his room and retired to their own suite for the night.

The next morning after Mikey and Coach Burnette boarded the shuttle bus with the other riders participating in the competition, Malcolm and Heidi had a late breakfast before renting a car and heading out for some shopping before the race. Since Mikey's qualification round wasn't until noon, they had plenty of time to drop some more cash into the Las Vegas tourism and hospitality industries.

Shortly before noon, Amir texted Kareem, saying "He's here."

"Excellent. Watch but DO NOT approach him," came the reply from Kareem.

Malcolm and Heidi reached the stands shortly before Mikey's qualification round, in which he ripped through the course, qualifying at fourth place among nearly one hundred of the most skilled riders in the entire circuit. Once the qualification rounds for each class were complete, there was an intermission preceding the national championship races.

During the intermission, Malcolm's phone buzzed in his pocket. Answering it on speaker mode, he said "Hey, Mikey!"

"Hey Dad. Hey Mom," said Mikey. "Did you guys catch the qualification round?"

"Of course, we did!" replied Heidi. "You were amazing out there!"

"And you qualified in the perfect position!" exclaimed Malcolm. "Great work, Son!"

"Any last-minute tips, Dad?" asked Mikey.

"Keep an eye on Daniel Greer." said Malcolm. "He's a sleeper, and even though he qualified two positions behind you,"

"He's holding back," said Mikey, finishing Malcolm's thought. "I know he's a better rider than any of the first three qualifiers, so I'll be keeping an eye on him during the race."

"I'm proud of you, Son," said Malcolm. "Excellent situational awareness, Mikey!" he added.

"And you looked so grown up out there on the track!" exclaimed Heidi. "I almost forgot you're my baby boy," she added, winking at Malcolm.

Chuckling, Mikey said "Well, I'm going to eat and go through my race prep. Wish me luck and I'll see you guys after the race."

"Good luck, Son!" came their simultaneous reply before the call ended.

Outside the track area, Malcolm and Heidi ate hotdogs and potato chips while wandering through the various vendor stands offering motocross paraphernalia and souvenirs. Amir shadowed them from a distance, unable to imagine how *that* man could have possibly overpowered Kareem's brothers and uncle, unless he'd taken them by surprise before killing them in cold blood, as the sole surviving ISIL fighter had claimed.

Shortly before the race, everyone poured back into the stands to cheer on their favorite riders. As the announcer introduced each competitor, the crowd would erupt with the cheers of their fans. When Michael Abernathy was introduced, there was a notable increase in the volume of those cheers which surprised even Malcolm and Heidi. As the cheers died down before the next rider's introduction, Malcolm caught sight of Kareem seated across from them on the opposite side of the track. He and his entourage had been enthusiastically cheering for Mikey, and it was obviously not an act for Malcolm's benefit.

With all of the riders positioned at the gate, the starting gun was fired, and they were off! In a spray of sandy dirt, the riders streaked out of the gate at full throttle. During the walk-through and again while watching his VR simulations the evening before, Mikey knew the track narrowed just ahead of the first curve, and only a handful of riders would be able to sneak through before being caught in the bottleneck. He attacked the curve aggressively, being one of the last riders to decelerate heading into the turn. As planned, he squirted through just ahead of the bulk of the riders, clearing the turn and avoiding the funnel trap. Exiting the turn, Mikey accelerated late, intentionally causing the riders behind him to slow, thereby creating a chain-reaction which literally stuffed the tight curve with an overage of riders. By the time that swarm sorted out their paths and emerged from the curve, Mikey and six other riders had taken a substantial lead over the pack.

From his position behind the leading riders, he patiently observed the manner in which each rider attacked the curves, whoops, hairpins, and the straight away. He also watched the preferred track positions of each rider when entering and leaving the turns and made mental notes of their techniques in hitting the ramps before each jump.

With the exception of one rider, Mikey knew how, when, and where to capitalize on the openings left by the other riders within the first three minutes of the six-minute plus one lap, race. The remaining rider was Daniel Greer, and he had been shadowing Mikey since the first time they emerged from the bottleneck turn.

At four-and-a-half minutes, he began swatting the competition aside, sweeping past them at the most unexpected times in some of the most inopportune and unforgiving areas of the track. At the six-minute horn, he was positioned right behind the leader with Daniel Greer stuck to his back tire like flypaper.

For Mikey, every race had always been a one-lap race consisting of four or five riders, at most. Those able to separate themselves from the pack would either rise and shine during the final lap, or crash and burn before it. During this final lap, he already knew where he would take the lead. What he didn't know, was how Daniel Greer would attempt to sneak past him before they crossed the finish line.

On the final jump before the turn leading into the last straight away, Mikey accelerated, hitting the ramp simultaneously and to the right, placing him on the outside edge of the track when approaching the sharp turn. During the race, Mikey recognized how a rider in that position made the leader uneasy when approaching the sharp turn ahead. The slight glance he made over his right shoulder was enough to pull him off of his ideal line when they entered the turn. Mikey, on the other hand, stuck to his line with iron resolve, hitting the curve so fast, it brought the crowd to their feet as they wondered if he could maintain his angle of attack without losing control and crashing into the outer barrier.

He did, and as Mikey exited the final turn into the whoops segment on the final straight away, neither of the two other riders were even close to him. Daniel Greer had made a similar observation while evaluating the leader's vulnerability, planning on exploiting it at the exact point where Mikey had. When Mikey shot into the position he'd been eyeing, he was unable to follow the line he'd previously plotted through the turn.

During the entire race and the weeks leading up to it, Daniel Greer had seen Mikey as the *only* person to beat. He knew Mikey was the best rider by far, and his only shot at winning would be staying close enough to him to force an error during the final lap of the race. For six minutes, Mikey had taken the center line on that particular ramp every single time. He'd hit it at exactly the same speed and angle each time, tending toward the inside edge of the turn following the jump. The line he'd taken on the final jump and turn combination was so at odds with his behavior during the rest of the race, that it left Daniel Greer bottled up behind both riders ahead of him, with no room to pass through on the outside, and travelling too fast to alter his course and overtake them from the inside.

All he could do was watch from his second-place position as Mikey danced across the whoops into the final straight away, taking the checkered flag and the national championship.

The crowd literally exploded into hysteria as Mikey crossed the finish line, and everyone along the course was on their feet, cheering at the top of their lungs. Across the track from him, Malcolm watched Kareem and his entourage practically going insane at Mikey's victory. What they were experiencing was genuine and their emotional response was undeniably real.

For his part, Kareem was ecstatic at having been present for the victory he had so clearly envisioned and predicted for Michael Abernathy. His respect for Mikey had grown ten-fold, and it was at that moment he realized using Mikey to execute a hollow vendetta against his father would be shameful and cowardly. Accordingly, he texted Amir, saying "It's over. We are done here,"

Amir did not respond.

Chapter Twenty-One

Amid the tumult surrounding Mikey's victory, Malcolm and Heidi were the proudest parents in the arena. After the final race category, all of the riders were invited to the press box for interviews and to describe highlights of their individual races. At fifteen, Mikey was the youngest champion in the group but had ridden the most flawless race by far.

After posing for photos and signing autograph cards for adoring fans, the next to the last person waiting to shake his hand was Daniel Greer. With a smile, Mikey greeted him saying "You are one amazing rider, Daniel!"

"Says the man who thwarted my plans at the last minute," replied Daniel with a wide grin. "I knew you were the man to beat, and you proved me correct. Excellent race, my friend!"

"Thank you, Daniel," said Mikey. "I'm sure we'll be seeing each other again, and often."

"Count on it!" said Daniel, turning to leave. "I've got a lot of studying to do, but you can be sure I'll be gunning for you next year, buddy." With a final wave, he was gone.

The last person in line was more excited than anyone else he'd seen all afternoon with the exception of his mom. He extended his hand to introduce himself, saying "My name is Kareem, and I am your biggest fan!

I've come all the way from Saudi Arabia just to see you race!"

"Wow!" said Mikey. "That's incredible! I'm just glad I didn't disappoint you!"

"Far from it," said Kareem. "You are a special young man, and I am honored to have met you."

"The pleasure was all mine," said Mikey. "I wish you safe travels and hope to see you again next year."

With a genuine smile and a nod, he turned to leave, only to discover Malcolm was standing right behind him. As the two men's gazes met, Malcolm smiled, extending his hand, and saying "As-salaam alaikum."

"Wa-alaikum-salaam," replied Kareem, accepting, and shaking Malcolm's hand before disappearing into the crowd of spectators exiting through the main gates.

Malcolm and Heidi remained with Mikey for several minutes before it was time for the team's shuttle to transport the riders back to their hotel. Departing with their UBER driver, they reached the hotel a few minutes ahead of the bus. After Mikey showered and changed, they would finally have a chance to share a celebratory dinner together. Unfortunately, when the bus arrived, Mikey wasn't on it.

Before the final passengers had even exited the bus, Malcolm said to Heidi, "Go to the room and lock yourself in. In five minutes, a man named Stewart will knock on the door seven times before saying only his first name. Let him in, and he will stay with you until Mikey and I get back."

Heidi was confused, frantically asking "Where is Mikey?"

"I know exactly where he is, and I'm going to get him, Sweetheart," said Malcolm. "They want me; not Mikey and trust me. We're both coming back tonight. I promise you."

Kissing Heidi's forehead, Malcolm said "Now, go!" seconds later, he disappeared out the lobby doors and was soon speeding out of the hotel parking lot in the rental car. Heidi rushed upstairs to their suite and locked herself inside, waiting for the seven knocks that would signal Stewart's arrival.

Amir Haddad had received Kareem's message but chosen to ignore it. Pretending to be another fan hoping to get a final selfie with Mikey, he suddenly pulled a gun, pointing it at Mikey's head, saying "keep your mouth shut, and you will be free within an hour, but if you scream, I will kill you where you stand."

Leading him around to the side of the building, he and Mikey piled into the backseat of a vehicle which then sped off down Boulder Highway, heading towards Henderson. Inside the car, he texted Kareem, before using Mikey's phone to text the coach, telling him he would be riding back to the hotel with his parents. Then he removed Mikey's GPS-equipped wristwatch and tossed it out the window. After a short ride, they turned into the parking lot of an old, boarded up bar with a sign out front that said, Ace in The Hole.

Amir had obviously been there earlier, judging by the broken lock on the back door. Leaving the driver outside to watch and wait for Kareem and Malcolm,

Amir entered through the storage room, walking down the short corridor which led into the bar area. Off to the right side of the room, there was a video camera positioned in front of a chair near the wall. Using Mikey's phone, he recorded a video message while looking into the camera.

"Mr. Abernathy, about now, you are probably wondering where Michael is. Don't worry, he's fine... for the moment," said Amir, panning left to show Mikey sitting on a stool at the bar next to him. "Oh, I used his phone to let the coach know you would be picking him up, so you were probably surprised when he wasn't on the bus." Feeling full of himself, Amir laughed while looking into the camera again, asking "Does your son know you are a cold-blooded murderer?"

Finally, Amir ended the message by saying, "I'm texting you the GPS location for the Ace in The Hole bar right now. I'm throwing a victory party just for Michael, and you are invited. You have twenty minutes to get here, and if I even think you've alerted the police, I will kill him without a second thought, and send the video of it to his mother! Fortunately, I have her number here too."

Amir ended the video and sent it to Malcolm. Afterwards, he shut the phone off and put it in his pocket before looking over at Mikey to say, "Well, in twenty minutes, we shall see just how much your life is worth to your father."

Without even looking at him, Mikey said "My dad is going to kill you."

Before Amir could respond to Mikey, Kareem entered the bar through the storage room corridor, saying. "Amir, what are you doing?"

"Mr. Kareem," said Mikey, surprised to see him. "What's going on? Why are you here?"

"That is an especially good question, Michael," he said before turning to look at Amir, saying "Release him immediately!"

Amir went ballistic, screaming "I will not release him, and you have no authority to give me such an order, Kareem! You are a pacifist coward, and you have brought shame on your father and on the name of your family!"

"It is you who are shameful, Amir; clinging to lies because the truth is an embarrassment to you!" said Kareem just as loudly. "They were my brothers, Amir! Not yours! Yet, you seek vengeance for a man—my father—who simply employed you! You have no standing, and it is you who have no authority to act in the name of my family! Now, let the boy go!"

Raising his weapon, he pointed it at Kareem, saying "You are weak, Kareem. You have always been weak, turning a blind eye to the injustice visited upon your family because you have grown soft. Your brothers..."

"My brothers were criminals!" interjected Kareem. "They kidnapped innocent children after killing their fathers and raping their mothers, because they wouldn't embrace their distorted views of Islam. Then, they corrupted our faith, twisting it into a weapon of war, when Islam has always been a religion of peace."

Shaking his head, he said "Now, you point your weapon at me, Amir, because I know the same truth that you know. After all, you have seen the same videos that I have seen! You have witnessed the crimes of my brothers as they tortured dozens of people falsely in the name of Allah, while you did nothing to stop them, Now, you dare to call *me* a coward!"

Walking over to Mikey and placing a hand on his shoulder, Kareem said "Go in peace, my friend. No harm shall come to you."

When Mikey stood up to leave, Amir fired a round from his weapon into the wooden surface of the bar inches from where Kareem stood. Afterwards, he said "No one leaves before Malcolm Abernathy gets here! He has fifteen minutes, and if he doesn't show up, I will kill both of you!"

The thing is, Malcolm didn't need fifteen minutes. By following the tracking device in the bracelet he'd given Mikey on their very first Christmas together, he'd seen them when they turned into the parking lot. Driving past it, he parked the rental car on the shoulder a few hundred feet down the road and jogged back to the abandoned bar, arriving fewer than ninety seconds after Amir, Mikey, and the driver did. He'd just finished stowing the incapacitated driver in the trunk of his own car when Kareem pulled into the parking lot.

Without a sound, Malcolm followed Kareem into the bar through the now unguarded back door. Just as he'd advised Mikey to do before his race victory earlier that day, Malcolm hung back, but remained within striking distance of both Amir and Kareem, prepared to kill both of them quickly and quietly if necessary.

"Malcolm Abernathy was trying to negotiate the release of the hostages taken by my brothers," said Kareem. "They abducted him, and brought him to the compound in chains, after stripping and beating him until he was unconscious."

"Lies!" yelled Amir. "He attacked them during their evening prayers and killed them without mercy!"

"How often did you listen to my father tell that lie, Amir?" asked Kareem. "He lied and sent men out to kill Malcolm Abernathy because the man *they* tortured, escaped and killed his brother and both of his eldest sons while still in chains, stripped down to his underwear, and bleeding from the knife wounds they inflicted upon him. I've seen the video, Amir! We have both seen it! Yet, you said nothing!" Shaking his head in disappointment, Kareem said, "It is you, Amir, who are the true disgrace."

Outraged, Amir lifted the weapon and pointed it at Kareem, saying "But, it is *my* story that will leave this shitty American bar tonight, because *your* story ends here."

Before he could pull the trigger, Malcolm's knife sliced through both of Amir's Achilles tendons. Having crept silently across the floor hugging the wall and concealed by the bar separating them, he'd come undetected to within inches of Amir, striking from the darkness like a deadly black mamba. Amir's legs buckled beneath him and he fired wildly into the ceiling while falling backwards onto the knife; the hilt of which was held firmly in place against the worn wooden floor by Malcolm's deadly hand.

Unsure of what had intervened, both Mikey and Kareem were shocked, staring in utter disbelief as Malcolm stood up, rising out of the darkness from the floor next to the dead body of Amir Haddad. Upon recognizing him, Mikey sprang towards Malcolm, wrapping his arms around him, saying "I knew you'd be here, Dad."

After a moment, Mikey and Malcolm turned to face Kareem. Unprompted, Kareem said "Go. This never happened. Both of you, go. My people will take care of this abomination, and your family will have nothing to fear from us any longer."

"Thank you, Mr. Amari," said Malcolm. "And may peace be with you always," he added, and he and Mikey turned to leave.

Before disappearing down the corridor, Mikey said "I'd still like to see you at the competition next year. After all, you are my biggest fan."

Nodding, Kareem smiled and said, "Thank you Michael Abernathy."

"Mikey," replied the younger of the two Abernathy men. "My friends all call me Mikey."

"Thank you, Mikey," said Kareem. "May peace be with you until we meet again, my friend."

Twenty minutes later, they were entering the hotel suite where Heidi was pacing the floor under the unquestionable protection of Malcolm's friend, Stewart.

"Oh my god!" screamed Heidi as they entered the suite together. "I'm so happy to see the two of you!"

she added, running up to, and wrapping her arms around both of them.

After a moment, Malcolm walked Stewart to the door, saying "Thank you, my friend. I'm not sure what I'd have done without you."

"That goes both ways," said Stewart, solemnly. "I take it, that's the end of our Damascus problem."

"Yes," said Malcolm. "Our slate has been cleared."

Nodding, Stewart said "Goodnight, Malcolm. Take care of that beautiful family, and the next time you're in Las Vegas, I'd like to introduce you to the wife and kids."

"Absolutely, my friend," answered Malcolm, before closing the door to the suite and leaning back against it, exhaling.

After a few seconds, he joined Heidi and Mikey in the center of the living room. At last, after so many years, it was finally over.

Chapter Twenty-Two

The next evening, Malcolm, Heidi and Mikey returned to Mountain Home, happy to be back in the arms of their peaceful little town. When they arrived at the house, they were barely inside the door before Coco and Bandit were all over them. Bandit evidently forgot he weighed 160 pounds while trying to leap into Malcolm's arms, and Coco was chasing an imaginary rabbit through and around their feet in an erratic figure-eight.

Despite ninety minutes of uncertainty, the trip had been amazing. Mikey brought home a national motocross championship trophy, and Heidi brought back half of the Fashion Show mall in the two additional suitcases she purchased. Of course, Malcolm was partially to blame for Heidi's purchases. There were simply so many things that looked amazing on her, he couldn't decide which ones to get, so he got them all.

They didn't even bother unpacking before turning in for the night. Everyone was so tired; they couldn't wait to fall asleep in their own beds again, and with Mikey starting the tenth grade on Monday morning, he had a big day ahead of him.

As always, Malcolm was up early to hit the road for his morning run, and while Bandit loved the dog-sitter, running seven miles with Malcolm was much more satisfying than walking a mile with the sitter, and having Coco stop at every clump of grass along the road to search for ladybugs.

During the run, Malcolm was more relaxed than he'd been in years, and everything around him seemed more vibrant and colorful than ever, as the first signs of autumn began creeping into the canopy of trees in the surrounding forest. Bandit's elongated stride allowed him to explore an even larger area than the mere seven-mile course covered by Malcolm so by the time they returned to the house, both of them felt energized and revitalized, and were ready to face the day that lied ahead.

After dropping of Mikey at school, Malcolm, Heidi, Bandit, and Coco arrived at their peculiar little shop in the now modernized strip mall, and before they even exited the truck in the parking lot, the security patrol vehicle was pulling up beside them.

"Welcome back, you two!" said Mr. Dyson through the lowered window. "How was your trip to Sin City?"

"Vegas was a blast," said Malcolm. "But it's nice to be back home. This little town has a way of growing on you."

"It certainly does," said Mr. Dyson. "In fact, my wife and I found a place right on the outskirts of the city and we're planning on moving here and renting out the house in Boise."

"Wow!" said Heidi. "Congratulations on your new place and be sure to let us know if you or Karen need anything."

"I'll pass that on to her," Richard replied. "I know she's really looking forward to the move. Now that I'm working here full-time, she says she doesn't see me *enough* anymore. Go figure!" he added with a perplexed grin.

"Well, it seems you've found the proper balance." said Malcolm. "We're glad to have you on-board with us, and we look forward to welcoming her into our little family."

"Thank you both," said Richard. "I'd better get going though. Most of the stores are about to open soon, so I'd better make another round to be sure everything is as it should be. You guys have a great day!"

As Mr. Dyson continued his rounds, Malcolm and Heidi opened up the shop and put on a fresh pot of coffee just a few minutes before Jupiter arrived. With a big smile, he said "Welcome back, you guys!" happy to see them both.

"Thank you, Jupiter," said Heidi, hugging him first, before Malcolm warmly shook his hand. "We've really missed you!"

"How was business while we were gone?" asked Malcolm, looking around the pristine shop. "Anything out of the ordinary?"

"Nothing I couldn't handle," said Jupiter. "A few small things, but all-in-all, it was pretty quiet." After a brief pause, he added "That was one hell of a race that Mikey rode on Saturday! It was certainly a nail-biter up to the very end!"

"You're telling me!" said Malcolm. "That young man is already a monster at fifteen, and he's only getting better!"

"Pretty soon, the girls will be beating down the door to get to him!" said Jupiter, winking at Heidi. "He looked mighty handsome up there holding that trophy over his head."

"Woah!" said Heidi, looking over at Jupiter. "Slow down a little bit! He's still just a boy and there'll be plenty of time for girls after he graduates from college!"

"I'm not the one you'll need to convince," Jupiter replied, raising his eyebrows. "The local news covered a couple of big motocross watch parties, and he seems to have a huge following from here to Boise, and on to parts unknown."

"Well, they'll just have to keep watching until he graduates then, won't they!" said Heidi, looking at Malcolm.

"Hey," said Malcolm, throwing his hands up in the air. "Don't drag me into this. It took me over forty years to find *you*, so I'm certainly no expert on courtship; however, if the right girl comes along, he'll wait as long as he has to. He's a patient young man, and his mother raised him well."

Before Heidi could respond, Malcolm said "Wow! Look at the time." Walking out of the office, he said "I'd better open up that front door. There's a lot of stuff out there somewhere that needs fixing."

After opening the front door, Malcolm stepped outside and looked down the rows of stores in the strip mall. The semi-ghost town had not only been revived; it had been born anew as every available space was now occupied with merchants and entrepreneurs breathing new life into Mountain Home. As he stood there smiling, Heidi approached him and hooked her arm into his, laying her head on his shoulder.

"You did this," said Heidi. "This is all because of you."

"We did this together," said Malcolm. "Without you, I'd have never thought to form a property management company to buy the place, and this mall would have faded quickly after the novelty of my bizarre little shop had worn off. You gave it meaning and depth and showed the world what only you could see at the time."

Looking up at Malcolm, Heidi said "That's where you're wrong, Sweetheart. This mall had been here for years, along with the people who drove past it every day with their broken things, and broken lives, and broken dreams. You gave them hope by showing them that just because something is broken, doesn't mean it has to stay that way. When you sit down with people, they bear their souls to you in the stories behind those dysfunctional things that they cannot bring themselves to get rid of. In taking the time to repair their broken things, what you're really doing is restoring the love they feel for those things and the memories associated with them. What you're fixing... is them."

Continuing, she said "I was broken when I came to you. I was afraid of everything and my fears were breaking Mikey too. Just watching you every day gave me a reason to believe in humanity again. You gave me a reason to believe there was more to me than the scars on my back, and the love you gave *me* so generously; you put into everything you do."

"Look around you, Malcolm," Heidi said, gazing with him down the shops along the sidewalk. "Everything you've touched here has bloomed into something beautiful, but the most beautiful thing of all, is right here!" she said, poking him over his heart with her index finger.

Smiling, Malcolm looked down at Heidi, taking her face in his strong but gentle hands and kissed her. As they turned to walk back into the shop, they noticed a young couple behind them, staring curiously at the sign above the door, as if wondering whether or not they should step inside.

When he and Heidi approached the couple, Malcolm noticed the distressed young woman was holding an ornate wooden box in her hands. With a smile he said, "Welcome to I FIX BROKEN THINGS. What can I fix for you today?"

As he ushered them into the shop, she handed him the box with a mixture of hope and frustration in her eyes. Looking inside it, a huge smile crossed Malcolm's face which visibly erased the fear from hers.

"I haven't seen one of these in years, but I know exactly what it's missing," said Malcolm, to her great relief. "Have a seat and let me grab my tools. In an hour, it'll be good as new."

A moment later, he sat across from the couple at his medieval looking workbench, rolling up his sleeves. Looking over to them, he said, "These things have been around for over two hundred years, and this one is in fantastic shape..."

The end.

RIANO D. MCFARLAND – Author Information

Riano McFarland is an American author and professional entertainer from Las Vegas, Nevada, with an international history.

Born in Germany in 1963, he is both the son of a Retired US Air Force Veteran and an Air Force Veteran himself. After spending 17 years in Europe and achieving notoriety as an international recording artist, he moved to Las Vegas, Nevada in 1999, where he quickly established himself as a successful entertainer. Having literally thousands of successful performances under his belt, *Riano* is a natural when it comes to dealing with and communicating his message to audiences. His sincere smile and easygoing nature quickly put acquaintances at ease with him, allowing him to connect with them on a much deeper personal level—something which contributes substantially to his emotionally riveting style of storytelling. Furthermore, having lived in or visited many of the areas described in his novels, he can connect the readers to those places using factual descriptions and impressions, having personally observed them.

Riano has been writing poetry, essays, short stories, tradeshow editorials, and talent information descriptions for over 40 years, collectively. His style stands apart from many authors in that, while his talent for weaving clues into the very fabric of his stories gives them depth and a sense of credulity, each of his novels are distinctly different from one another. Whether describing the relationship between a loyal dog and his loving owner in **ODIN**, following the development of an introverted boy-genius in **JAKE'S DRAGON**, chronicling the effects of extraterrestrial intelligence on the development and fate of all mankind in **THE ARTIFACT**, or describing an alternative world view as observed by a dog in **THE WORLD ACCORDING TO BANDIT**, *Riano* tactfully draws you into an inescapable web of emotional involvement with each additional chapter and each new character introduced. Added to that, his painstaking research when developing plots and storylines gives his novels substance which can hold up under even the staunchest of reader scrutiny.

Possessing an uncanny flair for building creative tension and suspense within a realistic plot, *Riano* pulls readers into the story as if they were, themselves, always intended to have a starring role in it. Furthermore, by skillfully blending historical fact with elements of fiction *Riano* makes the impossible appear plausible, while his intensely detailed descriptions bring characters and locations vividly into focus.

Although it's certain you'll love the destination to which he'll deliver you, you'll never guess the routes he'll take to get you there, so you may as well just dive in and enjoy the ride which is certain to keep you on the edge of your seat until the very last paragraph!

Made in the USA
San Bernardino, CA
21 May 2020

71902723R00132